SOMEDAY EVERYTHING
WILL ALL MAKE SENSE

Someday Everything Will All Make Sense

A novel

by

CAROL LaHINES

Adelaide Books
New York/Lisbon
2019

SOMEDAY EVERYTHING WILL ALL MAKE SENSE
A novel
By Carol LaHines

Published by Adelaide Books, New York / Lisbon
adelaidebooks.org

Editor-in-Chief
Stevan V. Nikolic

For any information, please address Adelaide Books
at info@adelaidebooks.org

or write to:

Adelaide Books
244 Fifth Ave. Suite D27
New York, NY, 10001

ISBN-10: 1-949180-91-3
ISBN-13: 978-1-949180-91-6

Printed in the United States of America

For my beloved son, Dylan Cormac

1.

Mother choked on a bowl of wonton soup. A tangle of bok choy, a larger-than-expected dumpling. A wayward thatch no one could foresee.

Asphyxiation is a silent but awful affair: the soundless yelps, the evocative hand around the throat (the universal signal for choking). The desperate pantomime, *help me.* I leapt to perform the Heimlich maneuver, driving my fist into the soft space underneath her breastbone, but I elicited only a pathetic hiccup.

"Breathe," I commanded, driving my fist harder.

The foreign body insinuated itself in the trachea, disallowing air passage. No words to communicate her distress. Like a harpsichord with a truncated disposition, certain notes impossible to sound.

"Mother!" I prevailed upon her. But it was too late. The foreign body had irretrievably lodged in her airway. My efforts to expel the wonton – desperate thrusts, imprecations to a heaven I only provisionally believed in – futile. An inadvisable blind "sweep" of the airway – contrary to all protocols for administering aid to a choking victim – drove the object deeper, beyond the grasp of my feeble digits.

Oh, Mother!

She was only sixty-two. It was a stupid way to die, and she did not even get to enjoy her General Tso chicken. The wonton soup was a free appetizer, included in the meal. The dinner special from Seven Happiness Chinese take-out: choice of entrée, wonton soup, $14.95 plus tax, guaranteed to arrive in under twenty minutes.

She did not eat her fortune cookie, which I opened long after the ambulance crew had left with my expired mother on a gurney. A crumbling oracle. It said: *Someday everything will all make sense.*

My girlfriend Cecilia is a therapist. She encouraged me to see someone, a colleague who specialized in traumatic bereavement. Dr. Fein and I discussed how American burial customs left the next-of-kin feeling estranged from the process of death, how mortuaries profited a tidy sum from their comprehensive packages (pick-up, embalming, pallbearers, tissues for the mourners), yet offered little solace to those left behind. She urged me to file a complaint with the Better Business Bureau regarding Mr. M., proprietor of M. & Sons Funeral Chapel, whom she believed subjected me to unnecessary and criminal stress in selection of the casket and bundling of mortuary services which by law were to be offered *à la carte.*
Dr. Fein nodded sympathetically, encouraging me to use the tissues on the table in front of me. "Do you think you're obsessively revisiting the incident?"

"Perhaps," I offered, not willing to discuss my preoccupation with Chinese takeout and the choking capacity of the menu at Seven Happiness.

"Next session," she leaned forward, "I'd like to review the incident in detail, so we can purge the negative content from your mind. It's very important in cases of traumatic bereavement. The experience will be cathartic."

I resisted. What was the point? So I could sit on her overstuffed leather chair, eyes shut, recounting the final moments of Mother's life? So that all of it could be dispelled with a wave of Dr. Fein's magic wand, no longer to trouble my sleep, to cause me to awaken, screaming, in the middle of the night?

I was not yet ready to banish Mother from my mind. If she continued to haunt me, what of it? She had been my mother after all, my only relation (I lacked siblings, aunts, uncles, not to mention a father), my confidante during long years when I aspired to be a harpsichord virtuoso, then settled for a post as an associate professor of musicology (medieval, Renaissance) at New York State University. It seemed only right that I should carry this memory with me, to remind myself of the precarious state we all exist in and to fan my anger toward Seven Happiness, whose sloppy cooking techniques were no doubt responsible for the "accident."

The "package" I bought from Mr. M. included use of a chapel for the viewing, a hearse for transit to the cemetery, and, of course, the casket – the "Eternal Bronze" model, top-of-the-line, satin-lined, to ensure that no maggots would disturb what the undertaker had wrought in his preparation room with his ungodly cements and embalming fluid.

The priest, whom I did not know, referred to Mother generically as "the deceased" or "the dearly departed," rather than by her given name, Celeste van der Loon. Henry Phipps, president of the Tudor Greens Society, lauded mother for her efforts with the spring plantings. Jose, our faithful doorman, cried, and remembered how Mother baked him an apple tart every Christmas. I wanted to say something, but could not: grief had stolen the words from my mouth, made me mute, unintelligible. My girlfriend explained that I was in shock, and everyone nodded sympathetically. It was Cecilia who recited the Twenty-Third Psalm, *Lo tho I walk through the valley of death*..... She also selected the attire for the corpse: a smart herringbone suit and pearls.

Before they closed the coffin, they allowed me one final moment with Mother. Her hands had been molded around a crucifix in a position of permanent benediction. She rested on a satin pillow, eyes glued shut, never again to look upon this world. Her hair seemed to me the only thing that had not been retouched by the mortician with his ghastly pan makeup and array of corrective creams. Her hair was freshly shampooed, a gentle shade of white. I stroked her hair and saved a lock. The rest of her, in reptilian fashion, had adjusted to the outside temperature (in this case, the chilly 60 degrees of the funerary chapel, the thermostat no doubt set to ensure optimal preservation in the days before burial). I refused to be assured by all of the usual platitudes – Mother was in final repose, she was in heaven among a pantheon of angels and saints, she was in a "better place," and would want me to "get on" with my life.

The drive to the cemetery was a blur. The putrid exhalations of the Long Island Expressway, always choked with traffic. Motorists with no respect for a funeral cortège tried to insert themselves between our slow-moving vehicles, honking, *honking!* to signal us to speed up, else let them pass.

Mr. M. unlocked the door to the stone crypt. The pallbearers laid her on the altar. Mr. M asked whether I would like to gaze upon the deceased one final time. Cecilia tried to dissuade me. Already hinting that I was "obsessing" over the physical manifestation of Mother, unduly interested in embalming procedures, etc., etc. I said yes, please. Mr. M. opened the upper half of the casket. Mother had shifted somewhat during transit. I readjusted the satin pillow under her head. I inhaled the smell of her hair, freshly shampooed. A fresh coat of mascara on her lashes. Patches of corrective cream that my tears, my copious tears, had washed away.

2.

In the weeks following Mother's death, I found myself stunned, staring into space, subsisting on nothing more than stale pastries, ghastly casseroles and a fruit tower of mandarin slices and sad, bruised pears.

I tried to pen some thank-you notes on the stationery provided by the funeral home. *Dear So-and-So, thank you for attending my mother's wake, great of you to come, thank you for the mass card and the cherry-filled chocolates. I have been stuffing my face with them as I howl in desolation.*

Dear So-and-So, it was so kind of you to attend the services at M. & Sons Funeral Chapel, thank you for the calla lilies and the generous subscription to the Harry & David fruit of the month. I am enjoying a kiwi as I write this.

Dear So-and-So, thank you for the sensitive words (May God save you, you look like a wreck), together with the tin of butter cookies.

Dear Mr. M. (or whoever it was who "prepared" my mother in the cold antiseptic room, head poised on a block while the life blood was drained from her):

Thank you for preparing my dear mother for burial, for steering me to the Eternal Bronze line of quality interment products. Thank you for holding my hand and allowing me to snivel on your cheap suit. It was unfair of me to accuse you (and your certified cast of morticians, cosmetologists and coffin salesmen, forgive my ignorance of proper job titles) of being interested only in the enviable economics of the business. People suffer, people die, people will always die.

I ripped the notes up and never sent them.

She was, according to the official register, DECEASED, no longer of this world, unmarked time, a hovering suspension, an overtone beyond the realm of audible perception.

Margin-less days, days when I hardly left the apartment, subsisting on stale peasant bread and preserves, wandering from bed to bathroom to bishop's chair, and back again, a recursive loop.

My only solace music. My harpsichord is a nineteenth-century Flemish instrument. I call her Aveline, after the heroine in a popular medieval morality play. She is not a Ruckers-Couchet (Flemish), nor even a Schudi (a slightly less reputable English instrument maker), but she has a tone I can only describe as otherworldly.

Some might find it difficult to understand my obsession with period performance. Why it is preferable to use plectra made from crow's quill? To tune the instrument in the quarter-comma meantone, the standard tuning of the era, rather than the equal temperament? The harpsichord, after all, is an obsolescent, dynamically-limited clavier, an instrument locked in one key; its popular descendant, the piano-forte, has no such strictures.

The Renaissance composer had to find beauty in the texture of the line, in the interplay of voices, in the use of hocket ("hiccup"); he could not, like the later Romanticists, change key, or burden chords with hideous extensions and inversions.

I had not played since the eve of Mother's death. I sat at the keyboard, adjusted the bench (my aging back prone to spasm and sensitive to the slightest differential in the bench's height), opened the brittle songbook, and played Guillaume de Machaut's *Ha! Fortune—Et non est qui adjuvat.* I translate from the medieval French:

Ha, Fortune, I am placed too far from port when you put me on the sea without an oar in a little boat, flat and without sides, weak, rotten, without a sail; and about (me) all the winds are contrary to bring about my death, so that there is no comfort nor salvation, pity, nor hope, nor means of escape. . . .

The text conveys the writer's desperation as he founders (literally) in rough seas. His flimsy boat has no sides nor sails and is rotting from within; waves threaten to overwhelm him; there is no hope of rescue. The only sure prospect is drowning; the bleak imagery of the stanza underscores the futility of our pathetic existences.

It might be said that I am inclined to melancholy, that my view of humanity (*i.e.*, man is frail and his nature essentially corrupt; there is nothing for us on this Earth save brief moments of transcendence) has been shaped by immersion in medieval texts and morality plays. Some might say – pointing to an obsession with sacred music and the principles of counterpoint – that I live in another era and am uninterested in the present day. Being unable to save my mother, to perform a maneuver so simple Heimlich himself says it can be "self-administered" or "performed by a child of six or seven" —- had left me hollow, unstrung.

Though Mother preferred the Romanticists – Beethoven, Brahms, and of course, Wagner – she understood my affinity for the contrapuntal lines of de Machaut and de Vitry. She would sip tea while I practiced the harpsichord, pausing now and again to give me unsolicited advice – *rubato*, or *un poco expressivo* – and on her face, eyes closed, lids fluttering, lips uttering silent incantations – I saw a look of rapture. I stumbled through to the end of *Ha! Fortune*, thinking that if I harnessed enough emotion, if I concentrated more on the text, if I executed the second strophe perfectly, I might summon Mother from the grave, or at least the apparition of Mother, something to convince me that she had, in fact, existed in this time in space, that she continued to exist, a parallel perfect interval, in another dimension.

3.

"Let's go out," Cecilia suggested. "You've been stuck in here for weeks." The manual on grieving advises that after an initial, intense period of mourning (sobbing, howling, wallowing piteously), the bereaved should not be allowed to sleep past noon. Do not permit him to fixate on the loss to the exclusion of all else, see obsessive grief response, Chapter 5.

"Luther!" Cecilia snapped her fingers in my face.

"I hear you," I replied, tossing the coverlet aside. In the distance, I heard the F# of a jackhammer.

"I'll run you a bath," Cecilia said, plugging up the drain and dumping essential oils in the bathwater. "This should be refreshing!" she enthused.

"Fine." I stumbled into the bathroom. I splashed water on my face, as if to convince myself that I was still alive, still here, so dissonant was the idea that I could exist apart from Mother.

The death literature states that it is important in the days following catastrophic loss to go about one's routine, to tend to personal hygiene. To eat healthfully, three well-balanced meals per day. Not to pick at the leftover General Tso in the refrigerator, no longer fat and juicy but a desiccated remnant of its former self.

"Do you want me to scrub your back?" Cecilia offered.

"No thank you," I replied. "And please shut the door so as not to let the steam out." I half-heartedly scrubbed with a loofah. Sad, flaking patches of skin floated to the surface.

"Are you okay?" Tending to the wounded, to the hysterically bereaved, had left her attuned to the frequencies of misery, the oscillations of despair.

"I'll be out shortly," I promised. I covered my face in a washcloth. I remained a while in the tub, contemplating the fact that I – scaly, dirty, fingernails ragged – was still alive, though Mother was not. Slurping broth one moment, dead the next. I removed the plug from the drain. The contents of the bath swirled down with a *whoosh*.

"Why don't we take a walk?" Cecilia suggested.

"I'm not feeling up to it," I replied.

She was unmoved.

"All right," I relented. I still had no idea, after fifteen years together, what she saw in me. Though by no means repugnant, I was not what one would call *traditionally handsome*. I have a prominent brow some might call looming, others (mean-spirited individuals, cruel children) have likened to that of a Cro-Magnon man. I have ears that protrude despite two operations to pin them back. I have a limp, a slight hitch in my step, attributable (specialists speculate) to my positioning in the womb, to the happenstance of one foot being tucked uncomfortably under the other, inhibiting movement. My sinus condition necessitates frequent irrigation with a saltwater solution and a Neti pot.

Cecilia started up the block, to the park where Mother and I ventured after dinner to discuss the day's events and to feed the pigeons crumbs from our repast.

"No." I yanked her hand back. "I can't go there." It is important to confront everyday objects and places, to forge a new routine, to adjust to life without the object of loss. Wait too long, and the mourner risks becoming "stuck."

"You can do it, Luther," she urged, cheerleader in times of grief and despair.

"I'd rather not," I said. I was unsteady, unable to stand on my feet. The world inspired vertigo, loss of equilibrium; without Mother as reference point, I was no longer able to make sense of anything.

"Good to see you, Mr. van der Loon," said Jose, outside watering the plants. He had been one of Mother's pallbearers.

I managed a wave. The sun was bright, too bright. The trees swirled, the edifices buckled: the rules of proportion warped and dissembling. I clung to Cecilia, my legs buckling.

A warbler sung off key. Pigeons flocked and scattered, sent heavenward by a backfiring truck. "You're doing great," she assured me, patting my hand.

My heart's rhythm *allegro vivace*. I took a deep breath, lungs filling with air, trying to establish a connection to the world outside of me: The dogs out for a mid-day walk; the office workers on lunch hour, eating their weighted salad bar selections.

Through gradual exposure, the bereaved can reacclimate to surroundings, to areas associated with the object of loss and the arena of death.

"We can stop here," Cecilia said, once we had reached the park's entrance.

I steadied myself on a lamp post. I remembered sitting on the benches with Mother after church as a boy, eating petits-fours, layered rainbows that I shoved into my mouth, licking fingers afterward. Oh, sugary paradise!

I trembled, unable to go further. Who would tend to the garden, now that Mother was gone? Who would organize the spring plantings? A day in the park with trowels, *Tannheuser* blaring. Who would solicit donations on behalf of the Tudor Greens Society? Who would scratch my back (as a harpsichord player I was required to file down my nails, leaving me helpless against the infernal itching caused by my flaking skin)? Who would brew chamomile, in the cracked blue-and-white teapot, scenes of the Orient and far-away places?

Hands around the throat, a desperate pantomime, I'M CHOKING, SAVE ME. An insoluble rune.

4.

"Mildred R. is still obsessing about whether she did the right thing by cremating Harold." Cecilia continued to see patients in 1C, her studio on the first floor, but since Mother's passing had lived together with me in 8C. "Have you ordered in yet?" she asked.

"No," I replied. Well she knew that I was engaged in a boycott of the Seven Happiness franchise.

"Luther, what are we going to do with this living room?" she asked.

I shrugged. I didn't want to bicker over a dead woman's personal effects, barter for this-or-that memento.

"We don't need to pack it all up now," she offered. "We can wait until you're ready to sort through it."

She entwined her soft fingers with my callused ones. It had been fifteen years since I had made her acquaintance during one of the annual planting events sponsored by the Tudor Greens Society. Fourteen years since our first date, at Jules bistro. Eating Provençal and conversing as the house accordionist inserted himself between us and demanded recompense for his awful rendition of *As Time Goes By.*

The date went well, despite the accordionist. Cecilia listened to me go on about my dissertation, never seeming, as many of my prior companions, to be dreadfully bored, even asleep, by meal's end.

You might have taken it as a sign, Cecilia, that I still lived with my mother despite the apparent means to move out; that I had no past relationships of note; that I carried a doggy bag dutifully home, containing not only the remnants of my fowl, but the untouched portions of your beef bourguignon (you, admittedly, professed to being stuffed!)

"To us!" I offered her a glass of Zwetzschgenwasser that I had decanted from Mother's hoard. It had a lovely fruity taste. (Mother loathed the American version of Schnapps, a vile, fruity concoction the consistency of cough syrup.) Cecilia threw the liqueur in my face and stomped into the kitchen.

"Cecilia! Come back here," I pleaded.

"Why?" She sobbed.

"Cecilia, I'm sorry if I offended you." Though possessed of perfect pitch, in matters of the heart I was, admittedly, tone deaf.

"Luther, I'm really trying. I've been there for you, I'm trying to help you with this process ("grief work": adjustment to life without the object of affection, an indeterminate period of lamentation and dysfunction). I know now is not the time (the grief-stricken, alas, are advised to focus solely on their grief and not to undertake other, major life decisions), but I can't help feeling neglected." She sniffled into a paper napkin.

I inhabited a world governed by Pythagorean ratios. Imponderable questions about diurnal commas and the nature of harmony. I had spent eight years in a monastery, studying brittle codices and subsisting on a vile gruel. I thought it romantic to serenade her with *Sic mea fata*, a monophonic love song that had been popular during the Middle Ages. "Cecilia darling, you know my feelings for you are genuine. Let's order from Marimba Sushi. They guarantee delivery in under thirty minutes."

"I'm tired of California rolls!" She sobbed disconsolately.

"You can order the yellow fin tuna. Or the wasabi-crusted filet. There are many other options."

"I'd just like to go out once in a while," she protested.

"I know, I know. I'll make it up to you, I promise. I just cannot bring myself to leave the sofa."

She announced that she was going downstairs to do some paperwork, and not to wait up for her.

I had put off proposing for years, for an indeterminate period of time some (Cecilia, her parents upstate in Ulster County, via malign missives), might call an "eternity." I lived in a world of illuminated manuscript and ancient tonal systems. I played period instruments sensitive to the slightest fluctuation in humidity, necessitating constant tinkering with their internal mechanisms. I spent eight years in southern France, living in an *abbeye*, working towards attainment of a doctorate in Renaissance music. Some might say I was not particularly attuned to the modern world, to the nuances of interpersonal relationships, to the notion that an engagement, never consummated, was like a sonata without exposition, or a symphony without a rousing finale.

I emptied the bottle of Zwetschgenwasser and, as seemed to be the habit on our anniversary, when I proposed a toast and nothing more, found myself consigned to the sofa, staring at the coffered ceiling.

5.

The new semester began at the university. I taught *Dawn of Musical Composition: Greek Modes through Renaissance Organum*. We studied the origins of harmony in ancient Greece; the rise of church music on the Continent; the ancient system of neumes, precursor to modern notation; and, of course, temperament. For the scale was not always divided into equidistant steps, based on the fiction of the equal-tempered "cent;" it was constructed according to the divine Pythagorean ratios.

The course was no longer mandatory, per Burt Lessing, chairman of the Music Department, but a mere elective. Burt deemed study of early musical practices a useless enterprise, relegating, with one stroke of his tyrannical pen, the entirety of Western music antedating Bach to a footnote.

The shortage of rooms in the Tishman Building had led to the relocation of certain classes (mine) to the Fenster Wing – home of the department of experimental biological sciences. Access to the building was frequently blocked by police barricade and a smattering of protestors.

The music department printout indicated that six students had enrolled in the course: five music majors and a doctoral candidate in medieval history. By half past the hour, only three had arrived. Two were found on the second-floor landing, trying to visualize a hidden door; the other had taken a wrong turn and was found stranded in the chimpanzee lockdown area, alone in a room of screaming primates involved in a language experiment.

Forty minutes of the class was spent in the dispatching of search parties and the extrication of William from the screaming recesses of the primate laboratory. I spent another ten minutes trying to locate a functioning outlet (one would think that a building dedicated to animal experimentation would contain enough outlets to juice up the industrial refrigerators, the electron microscopes, and the precision slicing equipment). I found a setting on the synthesizer that best mimicked a sixteenth-century Ruckers-Couchet, and began the lecture.

"Who here knows the difference between a perfect fifth and a tempered fifth?" I inquired, to blank looks. They, like all music majors, had been indoctrinated early on to believe that the modern keyboard reflected the available aural spectrum, that a major third (C to E, E to G#, and so on) was a major third and not hideously compromised by the "tuners" of the instrument.

"It is my intention to revisit the last three centuries of musical history. To posit that the way we hear music is based on a fundamental misapprehension about the nature of harmony. The problem of tuning is one that occupied the greatest minds of the Renaissance era, from Galilei to Kepler."

It was a tirade I delivered at the beginning of each semester. Generally, it was for Burt's ears – he, who thought it better to dispense with instruction concerning the "ancient" debates over harmony. I did not expect my students to appreciate that the very way they experienced sound was the result of artificial tinkering and an odious acoustical construct – the equal-tempered cent.

With three voices plus the piano, we sang Machaut's Lay mortel:

Do-lans cuer las, Di moy que fe-ras
Que diras, ou i-ras, Ne que de-ven-ras
Quant tu ver-ras, Qu'on ne te vuet pas
Plus n'a-ras, de sou-las, Que de dire "He-las!"

"Well done," I commended them. They had not butchered the *color*, or melody; they had stumbled only slightly over the medieval French; one could even sense, in the echoing silences, the resonance of the Just and perfect intervals. Divine proportions, etched in the sky and the elliptical motions of the planets.

"Next class, we'll begin at the beginning," I said, distributing the syllabus. "Just follow the signs back to the main building!" I chirped, trying entirely to forget the fact that my class took place in a building consecrated to animal experimentation. "See you on Thursday!"

6.

Returning home from work, I dared to pass by Seven Happiness Chinese take-out. The illuminated menu. The photos of sesame beef, Sichuan fried rice, cashew chicken, moo shoo pork. Behind the counter, the requisite poster for how to render aid to a choking victim. The usual traffic of rice buckets and dumplings in exchange for crisp American dollars. Nothing to alert the consumer of the fatal potential of the menu. Nothing to apprise him of the inadequately cooked wontons, of the dangers lurking in the murky broth.

Accident victims have their roadside memorials, their shrines of melted candles and teddy bears, RIP scrawled in magic marker. It did not seem right that Seven Happiness had no similar markings: no carnations on the sidewalk, no flickering candles. It did not seem right that customers could walk up to the counter and place their orders as if nothing had happened, nothing to alert them to the fact that a life had been lost, a life that might not have been cut short had some employee thought to observe proper food handling procedures.

Seven Happiness had only four or five tables inside. A few customers, generally eating alone. By far, the greatest part of its business was the take-out enterprise: bicycles were chained to a post outside, for hasty dispatch of orders. I recognized the worker who had delivered Mother's fatal meal blithely getting on a bike and pedaling away, plastic takeout bags in his metal basket. Come back, I shook my fist at him. Don't you know the tragedy you wrought? Don't you know?

But he was already pedaling down Thirty-Ninth Street.

I wandered into the bodega next door, bought some daisies, and left them on the pavement outside of Seven Happiness.

Bird on a briar, bird on a briar,

Mankind is come of love, love thus crave,

Blitheful bird, on me have pity

Or dig, love, dig thou for me my grave

In the lobby the following morning I chanced to bump into Adrienne La Planta, a fellow shareholder. She offered me her condolences, nodding sympathetically as I described, perhaps too graphically, the manner of Mother's death. She was a counselor-at-law and unduly interested in the minutia of the accident: Was my mother drinking at the time? Was she under the influence of prescription medication? Did she have a swallowing disorder? Was she trying to talk and eat at the same time? Was she eating in the usual sitting position? Did I perhaps save the rest of the soup or had I hastily discarded it? Did I partake of the soup? If so, did I encounter an impossible-to-chew wonton?

I enjoyed being able to discuss freely these topics, rather than receiving the usual grimace, the gentle reproach – Are you okay? Have you gotten help? The pained expression of the grief counselor, who tried to steer me into more productive areas, else purge the entire negative content from my mind via a marathon session of assaultive stimuli whereby the entire experience was stripped of import, rendered meaningless, so that I might return to the "business of the living." Given Ms. La Planta's professional calling, I recognized that her interest in Mother's death might well be pecuniary, her thorough dissection of the events leading up to Mother's death an informal case evaluation.

"If I may," she patted my arm. "I think you've suffered a loss for which you may be entitled to compensation."

"You think so?" I asked. I, of course, viewed Seven Happiness as the agent of Mother's death, in the same way Zarlino blamed his treacherous pupil Vincenzo Galilei for the demise of the mean-tone temperament, but I had not considered that Seven Happiness might be liable in the legal sense, that I might be entitled (as Ms. La Planta explained) to compensation for my losses, both in my individual capacity and as Mother's heir.

"Do you think she suffered?" Ms. La Planta inquired, head sympathetically tilted.

"I've tried not to dwell on that aspect," I replied.

"Of course, of course," she nodded, averting her eyes.

"The wonton became stuck in her throat and the life drained from her."

"Was she aware of what was happening?"

"Yes, yes, I'm sure of it. I could see it on her face. She clutched her throat. Shook her head. I tried to perform the Heimlich maneuver–" here I stumbled, "but was not successful."

"I'm so sorry. Terrifying," she commiserated. "I can assure you that you are entitled, as her distributee, to be compensated for her conscious pain and suffering. I know it's small comfort, but you can make them pay for your mother's suffering, put a stop to this irresponsible practice of dispensing wonton soup to the unsuspecting."

I nodded.

"Take my card," she offered. "If you're interested in pursuing legal action, just give us a call."

I looked at the ivory moiré card: Adrienne La Planta, Esq., Attorney-at-Law, Bloodstone & Moore, LLP. "Thank you very much, Ms. La Planta."

"Well, I'm off to court. I hope that you'll call. You really deserve to be compensated for your loss."

Her heels clicked across the floor.

That evening I told Cecilia about my encounter with Ms. La Planta.

"Oh, Luther," she shook her head, "she's just trying to take advantage of you."

"Why do you say that?" I demanded. "She was just offering her professional services."

"What good can come of this? It was no one's fault, Luther. Not yours. Not the Chinese deliveryman's. Not the short order cook's."

My fury mounted. "Well, whose fault is it then? Mother's? She should have foreseen that she would choke to death on a wonton?" My voice cracked.

"No, of course not," Cecilia said. "It's no one's fault. It was just a tragic accident."

"I refuse to believe that no one is culpable, Cecilia. In your universe we have only to go with the flow and accept what comes our way as Karma. Here, however, there was a clear agent in Mother's death, and that agent was Seven Happiness Chinese take-out."

"Luther, I'm just saying that I've seen patients go through this. They want to blame someone. They bring lawsuits. They're not able to progress through the stages of grief. It can be very destructive."

"I am not Arthur L.," I said, referring to a patient of hers who, following his wife's plunge from the northbound platform of the number 6 train, sued the City, the Metropolitan Transportation Authority, and Emergency Medical Services for failing to prevent her suicide or to restore her pulse.

"Are you listening to yourself?" she sighed. "You're obsessing. You're casting around, trying to find fault. Was the wonton too chewy? Was it indigestible....."

"With all due respect, Cecilia, those are valid questions." I recalled my enlightening conversation with Ms. La Planta, who informed me that negligent food preparation methods were responsible for thousands of deaths nationwide. Litigation was the only means of assuring that these purveyors of fast food and destruction obeyed the requisite food handling procedures and did not try to "cut corners," as she put it.

"Just don't jump into anything. You're in no position to be making decisions." What she meant to say was that I, having suffered recent, grievous loss, lacked certain critical abilities, among them the ability to function on a daily basis, the ability to rationally evaluate the circumstances surrounding my mother's death, the ability to engage competent legal counsel, if need be, to vindicate my rights.

"I just don't want you becoming stuck," she said, with a look of professional concern.

"I am not stuck," I assured her.

The doorman buzzed to inform us that the deliveryman from Sushi-on-the-Go was on the way. I grabbed some bills and waited by the door. The same way I awaited the deliveryman who brought Mother's last meal, handing him two twenties and letting him pocket a generous tip.

<h1 style="text-align:center">7.</h1>

I was experiencing complicated grief, or traumatic bereavement, a perversion of the normal stages of grief that had been outlined by Kubler-Ross in her seminal book on the subject, *On Death & Dying* (pub. 1969). A disproportionate grief response characterized by obsessive rumination over the manner of death. The persistence of intrusive imagery, to wit, the fingers interlaced around the throat, the desperate pantomime, *I'm choking.*

The sufferer is ever alert to the possibility of death, to the morbid eventualities of the everyday. He is in all likelihood familiar with the statistics concerning lightning strikes and other, random tragedies.

The survivor considers what he could have done. How he could have prevented the tragic incident (enrolling in Red Cross recertification seminars, practicing upon life-like dummies, memorizing the poster for *How to Render Aid to a Choking Victim*). How events could have turned out otherwise – e.g., she would have been less likely to choke if she had used a fork, rather than chopsticks, with which she was awkward.

The survivor is unable to take in enough air, literally feeling himself *choked up, choked off,* voiceless. It is common for the survivor to feel imperiled, to feel, keenly, the transience of life, to see the possibility of death shimmering everywhere, in pinched wonton wrappers and glistening broth.

The fabled "three delicacies" of the Shanghai wonton – pork, shrimp and meat. The precise equation of tragedy insoluble.

8.

After dwelling on the subject for a number of days (without consulting Cecilia – her opinion of the American system of justice was clear), I called Ms. La Planta's office and made an appointment for a consultation.

"If the lawyers think you have a meritorious cause," the secretary recited, in an uninflected voice punctuated by gum snaps, "they will represent you. You will not be charged a fee, either for the initial consultation, or for their legal representation, should they not prevail on your cause. If, and only if, the attorneys prevail on your cause, will they be entitled to a fee, one third of the proceeds, to be deducted from the amounts awarded in settlement or by a judgment of a court of competent jurisdiction. This message is in compliance with the tenets of the American Bar Association governing contingent representation."

"I understand," I said, hoping to stop the monotonous barrage.

"Can you come in tomorrow morning, ten o'clock?" the secretary asked.

"Yes, yes," I said. After weeks of wallowing, of howling, of feeling lost in the world, matters appeared finally to be moving forward.

The offices of Bloodstone & Moore, LLP, were located on the thirty-ninth floor of the Chrysler building. The waiting room overlooked Forty-Second Street from a calamitous height. A box of tissues had been strategically positioned on the coffee table. I perused a copy of *Tort Lawyer Today* – the cover of which was graced by two pin-striped crusaders, arms folded, superimposed against a stormy sky. I scanned the table of contents: "The Zone of Harm: Suing for Intentional Infliction of Emotional Distress"; "The Cancer Cluster: the Epidemiological Case"; "Municipal Liability in the Slip-and-Fall," "Suing for Wrongful Birth: the Emotional Fallout," etc., the scope of possible disasters and the size of the tort bar dumbfounding.

"Mr. van der Loon," the secretary snapped. "They're ready to see you now." She ushered me into a conference room where I was greeted by Ms. La Planta and several of her colleagues, Mr. Grunlicht (senior litigator) and Ms. Peppi (paralegal). Ms. La Planta urged me to have a Danish.

"Luther," Ms. La Planta stated, "I've spoken to my colleagues about your case. We just wanted to give you an idea of what you could expect."

"Of course," I said.

"Obviously, we're aware that your mother choked while eating the wonton soup from Seven Happiness Chinese restaurant. However, why she did so isn't entirely clear. Did she choke because the wontons were inadequately cooked? Because they were rock hard, impossible to chew? We need to construct a version of events that points the finger at Seven Happiness, but eliminates other possible causes, like your Mother choked because she was simply eating too fast, or not paying attention, or had a swallowing disorder, etc."

"I can assure you that she was the picture of health. Also, that she was always careful to chew her food."

"Good, good," Ms. La Planta continued. "From information we've been able to put together, preliminarily, it appears that Seven Happiness is considered a shoddy enterprise. They have a number of outstanding health violations. This adds what we like to call 'color.' Inspectors have cited them for the unsanitary qualities of the food preparation areas as well as for the presence of vermin. None of this means the soup was poorly prepared, but it certainly bolsters our theory that this was a sloppy operation where mistakes were likely to happen."

She took a gulp of coffee and went on. "Also, the length of time between food preparation and food delivery may have played a role. Wontons are known to rapidly cool and to become chewy. Seven Happiness uses only two delivery persons per shift; other Chinese take-out establishments in the area use five or six. Again, none of these factors is conclusive of guilt, but they paint a picture of an establishment willing to cut corners, to put customers' health at risk.

"If you give us permission, we believe we have grounds to institute legal action. We'll be suing Seven Happiness for pain and suffering and for wrongful death. How does all of this sound to you?" She leaned over, placed a hand on my arm.

"We've drawn up a complaint. We'll leave you alone to read it over. It's all the standard boilerplate, a lot of wherefores and whereases. Just make sure it meets with your approval."

It was hard to discern from the arch language and the circumlocutions what, exactly, I was suing for, though I'm sure that's why they were lawyers and I was a professor of medieval and Renaissance music. The ancient system of neumes, used to notate music until well into the thirteenth century, was more intelligible than the legalese employed by the attorneys to apprise the defendants of my complaint against them. I reached the final page. The *ad damnum* clause, informing the defendants that I was seeking in excess of $5 million in damages for my mother's wrongful death and conscious pain and suffering. It seemed a ridiculous amount. Yet no life was compensable in monetary terms, as Ms. La Planta was fond of remarking. I told the receptionist that I was ready to speak to the lawyers.

"I have decided, upon contemplation of the matter, to accept your offer of representation." I was uncertain of whether a flake of Danish was on my upper lip.

"We're pleased to hear it." Ms. La Planta shook my hand. Ms. Peppi affixed her notary seal triumphantly to the verified complaint.

I was finally doing something. Rather than wallowing piteously in my grief, I was undertaking a public crusade against the legion of take-out delivery establishments who would imperil the lives of their most loyal customers through undercooked and inedible fare. Others had railed against MSG and poisonous additives. Why shouldn't I have my day in court, my public service announcement, vindication for my suffering?

Ms. La Planta counseled me never again to step foot in Seven Happiness, lest I compromise my stance in the litigation; I assured her that I had been unable to step foot in the place since Mother's death. I crossed the street to avoid it; if I saw the neon sign blinking, I averted my eyes, not wanting to see the afterimage.

9.

"Cecilia!" I cried.

In my absence she had rearranged the furniture. Removed the petit point pictures of *la chasse* and medieval court life from the sofa (whip stitched in dear Mother's arthritic hand!), and lumped them in a corner.

The Schnapps was missing from the liquor cabinet. In all likelihood, she had emptied the bottle of *l'eau de vie* down the drain.

"Cecilia! What have you done?" I found it necessary to sit down, to steady myself.

"Nothing, Luther. I did nothing. I just rearranged some things."

"Nothing? You call this nothing?" I cried.

"Nothing is gone. I put the Hummels in your mother's closet," she explained.

"The–" I stuttered, "the Alpine chalet?"

"It's all in her room, Luther."

I rescued Mother's carved wooden back scratcher from the trash (excellent for reaching the underside of the scapula), and washed it under a stream of hot water.

"What are you going to do with that, Luther?"

"It's a memento," I countered.

Cecilia breathed in deeply. "I was just trying to help," she said. "It can be difficult to sort through a loved one's things. To let go, and imagine the world without them. There's no need to lash out at me."

What she'd wanted to say, no doubt: It's been months since your mother's death, and still, you stumble about. Neglecting basics of personal hygiene, forgetting to floss, scrubbing half-heartedly. You prefer to play Aveline, your nineteenth-century harpsichord, rather than spending time with me; you seek answers to the unanswerable in medieval codices (*Ha! Fortune*); you believe in the rules of counterpoint but question the existence of the Hereafter; you awake, frequently, in the middle of the night, waving your fist, cursing the legion of Chinese deliverymen in the City. You re-enact, in semi-consciousness, your pathetic attempts at the Heimlich maneuver (You wrote Professor Heimlich – still alive – to let him know you'd failed, *How did I go wrong?*). You break down, sobbing, at the end of the day (locked in the bathroom, ostensibly to run steam and drain the sinus passages), wondering how you will go on, how you can continue, day in and day out, day after day, when the fruit of the month turns from plum to pear and finally, to kiwi.

"I don't need your help," I said. "Please resist the impulse to rearrange the furniture, to empty out the étagère, to assume that this [here I picked up a replica, in miniature, of the Franconian rake, part of the Bavarian heraldic coat-of-arms] or this [here I waved a charming charcoal rendering of the Zugspitze, the "Matterhorn" of Bavaria] is meaningless kitsch. I would very much appreciate it."

They were just things, I knew, inanimate objects, but they were Mother's, and I was not ready to pack them up.

10.

Following institution of *Luther van der Loon v. Seven Happiness LLC and Bernice Wong, individually*, the franchise decided to exclude our building from the delivery radius. To stop shoving menus under the door. To deprive the residents of Harlequin Hall of their tasty moo shoo pork and steaming chicken and broccoli. The new menu, printed on glossy stock, depicted an X through the premises.

I stood mute in elevators while residents considered possible explanations. *Too many workers' compensation claims for bicycle collisions.* Or: *Charlie's Sichuan tipped off ICE.* Or: *A deliveryman must have slipped on the brass plate in the lobby.* This latter explanation seemed the most likely, particularly after Ms. Finnegan in 5B tripped on the very same plate while maneuvering a stroller into the lobby and threatened to sue. Everywhere one stepped there were unknown risks, unapprehended dangers, liabilities to be assessed by enterprising attorneys working on contingency fee.

Why must I go to the store to pick up my order? the residents grumbled. *Doesn't that defeat the entire point? Why can't I eat General Tso in the comfort of my own home?*, they railed, outraged that they could be refused something in this self-aggrandizing metropolis. Jose was sometimes dispatched with group orders, returning like a pack mule.

I could not help but feel misgivings. Qualms about suing a fast-food establishment for what might be called a freak occurrence.

But it was too late to turn back. Ms. La Planta informed me that withdrawing the suit would fatally undermine my credibility, make it appear as if I were a fickle, litigation-happy soul casting about for someone, *anyone*, to blame, as opposed to a plaintiff with legitimate grievances he was seeking to rectify.

11.

The world of Renaissance musicians did not turn on the 440 hertz standard. The octave had yet to be coerced into twelve equidistant steps, 100 cents apiece, facilitating the rampant modulation of the nineteenth-century Romanticists. Music was built from perfect, or Just, proportions: the octave (a ratio of 2:1), the fifth (3:2), and the fourth (4:3). The proportions divined by Pythagoras during his experiments on a gut-string lyre. Precise mathematical ratios reflected in the motion of the planets (*see* Johannes Kepler, *Harmoniches Mundi*).

But a problem soon presented itself, if not during Pythagoras' time, then certainly by the dawn of polyphony, in the thirteenth century. In theory, if one began on C and proceeded by fifths, C-G-D-A-E-B-F#-C#-A flat-E flat-B flat-F, one ought to arrive back where one started. But in practice, one encounters a howling "wolfe." The last interval – from F to C – inexplicably falls short. It is not a perfect fifth, but a hideous augmented fourth, otherwise known as the Devil's Triad.

Musicians attempted to avoid this dissonance at all costs – writing it out of their pieces, avoiding entirely the intervals B-D#, D-flat-F, F#-A#. But the existence of this foul interval underscored an inexplicable truth: Music was tainted by imperfection. The product of the ratios, perfect numbers, did not produce a consonant result.

12.

On Monday, a note was tucked into my box in the office ("Mr. Lessing needs to see you"). I made my way to the ninth floor of the Tishman Building.

"Ida." I nodded to his secretary. She inserted a sheet of paper into her typewriter and expertly aligned it. Well into her seventies, she favored short-hand and carbon ribbons and other, obsolete office messaging systems.

"Luther." She rose from her desk and made her way toward me. I had grown accustomed to people flinging their arms around me, pulling my head to their shoulders, and encouraging me to "let it all out." During the brief service at M. & Sons I had soaked the lapels of many a well-wisher. "I am truly, truly, sorry. I know how difficult this must be for you." She looked at me. Her glasses had the effect of magnifying her teary eyes. "Did you get the fruit basket?" she asked.

"Yes, yes," I assured her, though I could not remember signing for *a gift for you from your friends and colleagues in the Department of Music*, removing the crinkly cellophane and gnawing on an apple, or pear, or grapefruit, or whatever fruit of the month it contained.

"I wanted to order a giant basket with salamis and caviar and French cheeses but Mr. Burt," she lowered her voice, "is such a cheapskate. *You* know. What can you do? It came from the Gotham Fruitier," she informed me. The establishment was, apparently, in the business of upscale funereal arrangements, providing an endless supply of fruit and non-perishable crackers to appease the palate and sate the gnawing hunger of the grieving and the bereft.

"It's the thought," I replied.

"I lost my own mother last year," she said, lowering her eyes, describing in minute detail, with interpolated exclamations (*It was awful! I was so traumatized!*) how the nursing home had refused to recognize her power-of-attorney to decide such matters as *viz.*, nutrition and withholding of same; how the nursing home, contrary to her express wishes, *inserted a feeding tube into a ninety-nine-year-old woman!* and *proceeded to try to revive her when she coded!* Ida hung her head, recalling the entire disturbing episode, including the insensitive comment of one nurse that she was in effect "starving her own mother" – was that what she wanted?

Since Mother's passing I had been privy to such confidences, intimate accounts of terminal cancers, irreversible comas, fatal aneurysms, and sudden accidents (The car came out of nowhere and jumped the median! They couldn't get her out, and had to use the jaws of life – the jaws of life! – to extract her). Others projected onto me the thumbnail sketches of their own, tragic losses.

"I know she's better off." Ida cleared her throat and wiped away a tear. "But it's still difficult, you know. *You* know," she emphasized, acknowledging that I had been initiated into this bereft society, this company of the grief-stricken.

I nodded as solemnly as I could. "Thanks again for the kiwi," I reiterated. "Is he in?" I asked, nodding towards Burt's office.

"Yes, yes. Go on in."

Burt had recently returned from a meeting with the "big donors," titans of Wall Street and industry who promised a few pennies to the arts for every dollar they plowed into the school of business. "Do you want one?" He unfurled a cocktail napkin containing some lurid red shrimp, doused in cocktail sauce, and a fistful of chafed *crudité*.

"Thank you, but no thank you." I had been stricken, once, by a festering spinach dip at a faculty *soirée*.

"We need to discuss the arrangements for the upcoming Early Music Symposium." Our department had sponsored the gathering of musicologists and period music aficionados for fifteen years running, following the death of its previous organizer, a lute-playing monk at the University of Gstaad. "Are you sure you don't want a shrimp or something? A mini frank?" He held up a tiny, bloated sausage that had been impaled on a plastic spear.

"No, no." I held up my hand.

"You know I've tried to accommodate this function over the years, but funding is down and we need to be, uhm, more austere."

We were forced, yearly, to enact this ritual: I to beg for funds, to plead for faculty housing and a wine and cheese reception; he to make me grovel, to promise to teach an extra section of sight singing and dictation, drilling the students to recognize the intervals I opposed on moral principle, fooling their ears into thinking a major third was supposed to be 400 cents, as opposed to the divinely ordained 386.31.

"If faculty housing is unavailable, participants can stay in the dormitories."

"I'm afraid that's not going to happen." Following an incident, last spring, in which a visiting professor of anthropology had exposed himself to several frightened co-eds, the students had shut their doors against lecherous adults. It was unavailing to argue that a Professor of Medieval Music, a scholar who had spent the better part of his professional career locked in the temperature-controlled halls of the *Bayerische Staatsbiobliotek*, was not the equivalent of a lascivious anthropologist who studied tribal sex practices.

"Where are they going to stay then?" I pleaded.

"I'm sure you can get a group rate at an area motel," he replied. "There's another thing." Burt shifted in his chair, puckered his lips into the leering *embouchure* I recognized from faculty concerts. "We're hosting another collegium this year, and unfortunately it's scheduled for the same week. Nothing I can do about it, I'm afraid. There's plenty of extra space in the Fenster Wing."

"The Fenster Wing!" I bellowed. "How will we get the instruments inside?" I despaired.

Burt dragged a celery stalk through ranch dip. "You can get some students to help. There's a back window, too. Maybe they can rig something up." I thought of my precious clavicytheriums, my virginals, dangling perilously from pulleys, wavering over a courtyard in which they no doubt disposed of animal excrement and the remains of "sacrificed" animals.

What other indignity could I endure? I would have to investigate block room rates for the Best Western on the far west side of Manhattan. I might be forced to lodge my colleagues in an airport motel and transport them daily in a hideous minivan into which we would somehow need to stuff ten surly professors and their strangely configured instruments, upright virginals and arched neck lutes sensitive to the slightest vibration, let alone the potholes on the Grand Central Parkway. Rather than a breakfast buffet in the Tishman Building vestibule, participants would have to choke down croissants and mini-bagels in the halls of the vivisectionist wing, fearful that an escaped chimpanzee (those not immobilized in a vice somewhere) might make off with their sliced cantaloupe.

The Professor of Medieval and Renaissance Music, a practitioner of an obscure discipline, devotee of obsolescent instruments with strange configurations, did not have much bargaining power.

"Very well," I acquiesced, stabbing a mini frank with a garlanded toothpick.

13.

Cecilia suggested an after-dinner promenade. "Very well," I agreed, loosening my tie, forgoing tweed jacket, and changing into a pair of breathable pants.

The neighborhood has not changed much since my youth. A cluster of Tudor revival buildings, constructed in the late nineteen-twenties. Fred Finch chose the spot – a stretch of the East River waterfront in the Forties, long neglected due to unsightly runoff from brothels, barrooms and slaughterhouses in the area – to erect one of the City's first planned developments.

I was born here, in the year of our Lord, *annus domini*, nineteen seventy-five, and I will likely die here, prematurely (speeding taxi, lawsuit-worthy fall off a crumbling parapet) or not (heart attack, stroke, dementia that would make a tapioca pudding of my cerebral hemispheres); in the meantime, I would continue to live in 8C, the apartment Mother had bequeathed me, trying to fend off maintenance increases, and subsisting on the measly stipend afforded me by the university.

Cecilia and I followed our usual route. We walked up the block toward Tudor City Place; from there, we turned left, past Forty-Second Street, finishing our perambulation in the gated north park.

Many of the benches had been dedicated, via discreet bronze plaque, to the memory of a deceased loved one: a spouse, parent, or child who had vanished into the ether. I surmised that they were running out of space for these *memento mori*, for of late the plaques had appeared unexpectedly underfoot, on the cobblestones ringing the flower beds, at the foot of trees, dedications at once poignant and horrifically sad.

Cecilia sensed my apprehension, and guided me to one of the benches. I avoided looking at the plaque, not wanting to efface the memory of someone's mother with my lumbering physique, which after years of period performances had grown stooped, weary, warped in the lumbo-sacral area, nerve-root derangement at the level of L5-S1.

"It's okay," she said, patting my arm, offering me a shoulder if I wished to weep, clandestinely, it still being difficult for me to acknowledge the loss. "It's okay to talk about her; it's perfectly natural that this setting would stir emotions in you. Your mother, after all, was instrumental in the preservation of these parks." In the nineteen-seventies, shortly after I was born, a ruthless developer tried to buy up Tudor City's parkland, hoping to erect what would assuredly have been a glass-sided eyesore, had Mother and her coterie of preservationists not intervened. They had not wanted the parks to go the same way as the tennis court, which had been demolished in the nineteen-fifties, the land consecrated to a behemoth red brick apartment building of incongruous mid-century architecture.

"It's just," I faltered, having difficulty finding the words to express the sentiment, no words adequate. "In any event, I'm sure you hear enough about this during office hours. You must grow weary of it."

"Luther," she looked directly at me, "I'm here for you. We're in this together. You're my life partner," she reminded me.

"Nonetheless, I'm sure it's tiresome." Tiresome to hear the lament, the yearning for the object of loss, the outrage at her precipitous departure. Enervating to sort through a loved one's belongings, arrange for charitable donation, feeling guilt for throwing out the most trivial memento, the most ghastly Hummel in the collection. Difficult to be so excruciatingly polite, to be at the ready whenever a torrent of emotion threatened to unleash itself, like a tickling in the nostrils that will not be appeased until there is a violent, expulsive sneeze. And the tirades, the endless tirades, against M. & Sons Funeral Chapel – I had just received a supplemental bill for "extensive cosmetic correction," whatever that meant.

When a note is plucked, the listener hears not only the struck tone, but those shimmering above – what is known as *the overtone series*, the fifth, the fourth, the octave, and so on, in the ratios described by Pythagoras. In a real sense, a musical note contains within it all the tones of the spectrum, the glimmering light of far-off musical universes, infinity expressed in one, resonant note.

I gripped Cecilia's hand tightly.

"It's okay, Luther." She patted my hand.

Mother, so recently a part of this world – planting bulbs in the north park, complaining about allergy season – was no longer respiring, had left the mortal sphere, and now inhabited some invisible realm beyond my apprehension.

14.

I went to Rolf's Biergarten. A slice of Bavaria in Kips Bay. An incongruous wood frame chalet; a *trompe l'oeil* of Alpine mountain villages. Servers wore full skirts and peasant blouses, cinched at the waist; the beer steins said *wilkommen.*

Oktoberfest was in full swing. The proprietor recognized me and said it was "on the house"; he had always been fond of Mother, having grown up in a Bavarian village not far from hers. The two often reminisced in the German tongue, a language in which I am not fluent. I remembered to place my verbs in the second and final positions of the sentence, but struggled always with the cases, the dreadful prepositions which changed according to the gender of the noun and rendered speaking, for the nonnative, a linguistic trap. I wished now that I had applied myself more diligently to my *Workbucher*, so that I might reminisce with Mr. Mueller, to share our vivid recollections of Mother, who held her alcohol better than any man with a hundred pounds on her.

Mr. Mueller held a beer stein aloft and bade me to drink up. I obliged, drowning a pitcher in under two hours. The murals of plaited Alpine lasses, once cutely kitsch-y, seemed sad. *You will all grow old and die*, I spat at them. *Ich bin hier*, I shouted, though no one could hear me above the din. I gulped down cold potato soup, Mother's favorite, as if therein I could discern something of her, something tangible, a whiff of skin or the dew of breath. I choked down the soup and set it aside, to wallow in my beer stein.

"Ein bier, bitte." I motioned to Mr. Mueller.

"Are you okay, son?" he asked me.

"I'm fine, just fine," I assured him.

"We all miss her." He patted my hands, my gnarled hands, warped from years of communing with a seventeenth-century instrument, the tip of my fourth metacarpal missing after an unfortunate accident in which the finger had become ensnared between case and clavier. Mother had come to my rescue, directing me to bite on a rag soaked in Schnapps while she extracted the imperiled digit. Had she not acted quickly, I might have lost the entire finger, not merely a tiny portion of the tip, effectively ending my career as a harpsichord virtuoso and interpreter of Renaissance troubadour repertoire.

You had saved me, Mother, but alas, I had failed to save you, unable to perform the Heimlich maneuver, a simple matter of applying steady upward pressure just under the breastbone, causing the foreign body – POP!—to be ejected. I put my head on the bar. Other patrons sang *Drink, Drink Little Brother, Drink*.

"Your mother was a fine woman," Mr. Mueller said. "We went back a long way." I sensed that he wanted to say more, but for limited English and a sense of posthumous propriety. I remembered him from the funeral home, genuflecting to say a prayer on the padded kneeler, placing a carnation inside the Eternal Bronze casket, saying, like most of those assembled, *If there's anything you need, just ask*, inscribing his name in the book of mourners, taking a laminated prayer card, Celeste van der Loon, Our father and the heavenly host, pray for us.

"Well, she's gone now." I gazed at the ruined frescoes of Alpine bliss, the chiaroscuro of the Matterhorn and the River Rhine.

"Let me get a cab for you, son," he said, ushering me outside. He said how highly she had regarded me, her only son and relative, doctor of musicology, harpsichord virtuoso, author of a monograph on Silbermann's Sixth Comma meantone, devoted son, *devoted son*, a boy who stayed, long past adulthood, a *rallentando*, a long *diminuendo*, sharing her solitude and fondness for bittersweet chocolate. He patted me on the back, and held the hair from my face as I was stricken curbside, regurgitating chunks of potato soup and a bilious stream of hops.

Tense negotiations ensued with a cab driver. He had witnessed the entire incident – the vomitus, the stream of regret – and refused – despite Mr. Mueller's assurances, and the driver's sworn promise to take the passenger anywhere in the five-borough area (appearing prominently on the posted bill of rights) – to transport me fifteen blocks north to Tudor City. He insinuated that I would befoul his rear seat, leaving the cab with an odor that could not be eradicated by the pine air freshener dangling from the rearview mirror. "Impossible to get the smell out," he lamented, relenting only when Mr. Mueller assured him that I would keep my head in a plastic bag for the duration of the ride, averring that I would rather smother in my own vomit than ruin the leatherette interior of his vehicle.

We proceeded north – or so I gathered, having no perspective, no view save that of the interior of a supermarket shopping bag. He told me to "hold on" to the flimsy strap in the rear as he sped up the avenue.

"Here," he said, depositing me on the corner of Forty-First Street, opening the windows to air out the vehicle before driving north into the night.

I rang the bell for a good five minutes before rousing Jose from his slumber. "Are you okay, Mr. Loon?" (unfamiliar with the Germanic prefixes, he simply truncated my surname).

"Quite all right, Jose," I lied. (I was not aware, until examining myself later in the frank light of the bathroom, that my shirt was soaked through, a boiled potato stuck to my collar.) "It's Oktoberfest," I informed him.

"I did not know, Sir. Can I get you something?" he asked.

"No, nothing," I assured him. My apologies in advance for smudging the brass plate you so assiduously polished with my grubby hands, for marring the French wood paneling of the elevator with my projectile vomit.

I stumbled into the apartment, taking care not to awaken Mrs. Hildebrandt next door. She had nothing to do but engage in letter-writing campaigns with the board of directors, complaining about insufficient heat, the clanging in the pipes, her life devoted to close scrutiny of the building systems and the hidden exhalations of the building.

"Go back to sleep," I mumbled, turning the key.

I wandered into the kitchen. I kept in the drawer the tattered menu from which Mother had selected her last meal. She had circled No. 25 – beef and broccoli, then erased it, changing it to No. 29 – General Tso chicken. The faint ring around the former a penumbra of what might have been, had she not been stricken at the last minute with a desire for General Tso. Was Number 29 less auspicious than Number 25? Had she, by effacing her prior selection and selecting at the last minute Number 29, changed the order of the universe? The invisible shimmering patterns? The wavelengths of Fate and Providence?

Number 25 was an *à la carte* selection, whereas Number 29 was listed among the "dinner specials," bargains that included choice of spring roll or wonton soup. Had she chosen the former, she would have never encountered the steaming plastic container of wonton soup, never inhaled the contents – the autopsy report, subpoenaed by my counselor-at-law, indicates that she aspirated wontons and ruinous bitter greens. She would not have fallen, helpless, to her knees, whereupon I, would-be-rescuer, would fail in my efforts to perform the Heimlich maneuver.

What was the derivation of the name Seven Happiness? Did it signify that there were seven heavens or afterlives? Did it refer to an earthly level of happiness? Should it have been pluralized, though happiness appeared to be an unquantifiable noun and therefore fixed in the singular?

I could not bring myself to throw the menu out. The evidence of her hand upon the paper. The hesitant circle, followed by the decisive ring around General Tso chicken, her final selection, a meal that would lay cold in its plastic takeout container, long after the ambulance crew had left with my expired mother on a gurney.

15.

I watched a six-part series on burial practices on the Public Television Station, W-NET. The Chinese bury their ancestors under their houses, believing that the spirits of their dead loved ones will animate and guide them in their everyday lives. The Hindi burn their dead on funeral pyres, in ceremonies conducted by the eldest son; a sect in northern California commits their dead to the ground in burlap sacks, hoping to compost their loved ones.

"Stop watching this, Luther." Cecilia interrupted me during a particularly disturbing segment on the Zoroastrians, who let their dead languish in heaps in silent towers, called *dakhmas*, where they are languidly picked apart by the vultures.

"Please, you're standing in front of the television."

"What purpose does this serve?" she pleaded with me.

"Did you know that the Zoroastrians consider the dead to be untouchable? At the moment of death they are contaminated by the spirit of the corpse demon. No one is allowed to touch them. The body is considered corrupted. They throw it on a heap–"

"Enough, Luther. You're tormenting yourself. You need to know every gruesome detail of the mortuary. How they prepare bodies for embalming–"

(N.B., a mortuary assistant makes a discrete incision in the carotid artery and pumps it full of embalming fluid, displacing blood and drainage via the jugular vein.)

"If they don't have enough vultures, the bodies lie there, in a slow state of decomposition. They need the vultures to hasten the process. They like the eyes. The eyes are a delicacy."

"It's not productive. If you could see what happens in the mortuary, would that bring her back? Would it help lessen the loss?"

"They make special dispensation for the temple assistant. He rakes the bodies every few days to ensure that they are decomposing at a steady rate."

"Luther!" she screamed in my ear, an unnerving pitch in the ethereal registers of the piano. "You're not listening to me. You're intellectualizing your grief. You can't express your grief, so you're obsessing over burial customs."

How could no one care about these things? How could they entrust their freshly dead to the mortician, confident in his embalming methods, trusting in his dignified treatment of the body, certain that he was not desecrating their loved ones in his preparation chamber, or, God forbid, engaged in one of those body parts rackets in which bones were broken off and trafficked to tissue banks, the pilfered bones replaced by PVC piping, the post-mortem incisions hidden under burial attire and a satin blanket.

I had nightmares, still, of the casket room: the shelves of coffins, ranging from the visibly cheap to the garishly expensive; finishes of polished mahogany, gleaming steel, and eternal bronze; satin-lined, with pillows and blankets to conceal the hideous drainages that in time would mar the interior. The mortician encouraged me to feel the satin lining of the Eternal Bronze line, steered me to the top-of-the-line model, and otherwise urged me to "do right" by Mother's corpse. Alone with Mr. M., in shock, I capitulated to the purchase of an Eternal Bronze casket with silk lining, a cozy blanket, and a gold-plated crucifix to serve as an object around which the deceased's hands would be lovingly arranged by the professional staff at M. & Sons.

It was not what I wanted. I wanted to wrest Mother's body from the preparation room, where it was systematically being drained of blood through a discrete incision in the carotid artery. I wanted to carry her to the River Rhine, to bury her on a flowery bank in the land of her youth (though I knew, in some hideous part of me, that the body would not survive the seven-hour flight in unpressurized cargo). I wanted to commit her to the ground of the north park, so that her decomposing body could nourish those very same blooms she had so lovingly tended. Some societies heap their loved ones on bonfires, the eldest son reciting incantations to release the spirit to the next level of existence. Some societies commit the deceased to pine boxes and bury them before they began extruding. Members of our society, constrained by certain health and sanitation laws (no doubt lobbied for by the death care industry) were precluded from burying or otherwise disposing of their own loved ones. It was a misdemeanor to dispose of a body in an unregulated manner, which meant that no one other than a licensed mortician was allowed to embalm the deceased or to inter the beloved in a grave.

"If I want to 'obsess' about burial customs, then I will! You," I pointed at Cecilia, "know nothing about what I feel. You've never had to entrust a loved one to a certified mortician, taking it for granted that he'll treat her with dignity in the hideous back room." ("Off-limits," the sign read, to dissuade the grief-stricken from wandering in and viewing the corpse in a state of shocking repose, lips agape, eyes glazed over, limbs so stiff they had to be 'massaged' before the corpse was dressed – yes, Cecilia, I had devoured Ms. Jessica Mitford's charming chapters on decay and decomposition in *The American Way of Death*.)

"I may not have experienced a similar loss, Luther, but I can commiserate. I've seen many patients through this difficult period. Why don't you just let it out. Have a good cry."

"It is a misdemeanor for me to handle my own mother's body, to prepare her for burial, even to see 'corpse preparation' – lest I violate laws of sanitation and decency. Why is someone with an associate's degree in mortuary sciences permitted near my mother, while I am shut out, left to wonder what hideous desecrations of her person have taken place in their secret chamber, what orifices they have sewn shut, what rigid limb they have broken off and jammed into a stocking (Was she even wearing stockings? I wondered. Or underwear, for that matter?)"

She grasped my hand tightly. "We'll get through this, Luther," she said, positioning herself in front of the television so that I missed the last segment. "It'll just take some time."

Seven Happiness changed its take-out menu. (I grabbed one from the outside bin and hastily ran down the street, looking both ways to ensure no one had seen me.) It had a new glossy cover and renumbered selections. General Tso was now number 31; Peking duck, number 22. Wonton soup had been eliminated from the menu, both as a stand-alone selection and as a complementary appetizer. Wasn't this exactly the evidence of guilt that we needed? Recognition that their wonton soup had been the agent of Mother's death? I called Ms. La Planta, eager to impart the news.

Her response, however, was less than encouraging. "It's evidence of nothing, Luther. It's the equivalent of a post-accident repair. Inadmissible. It can unfairly influence a jury."

"Precisely, precisely!" I exclaimed.

"But if the law allowed that, no one would ever undertake remedial measures. Fixing something would be tantamount to an admission of guilt. That's bad public policy."

I thanked Ms. La Planta for the legal education and hung up the phone. In frustration, I tried to shred the menu, but the glossy stock on which it had been copied proved difficult to rip into shreds.

16.

Group piano was scheduled at eight o'clock in the morning. Play a scale. *Do-re-mi.* Like the cranial vise of the vivisectionist, *la-te-do*, increasing pressure.

Now let's transpose the formula and start the scale on G.

The class objectives, as detailed in the syllabus, were to instruct the music student in basics of keyboard technique and theory, to impart fundamentals of harmony and melody, and to reinforce skills learned in sight singing and dictation. I stuffed my ears with cotton and prayed that the hour would pass with my sanity intact.

I put page one, volume one, of Modern Keyboard Classics in front of them, counted off a beat.

I wheezed out a sad stream of coffee from the machine in the faculty lounge. I looked over a tray of scavenged mini bagels and muffins, contenting myself with a bit of unmolested crumb cake.

The Department of Music was not the School of Business, with its gleaming marble floors; it was not the School of Law, with its alabaster statues of weighted Justice; it was not the library, with its checkerboard floors and ascending stacks of books, Escher-like, as far as the eye could see (N.B., the library had been the situs of several suicides, or drinking accidents, an unfortunate combination of floor pattern and open atrium design). The Department of Music was not the recipient of the university's largesse; it had no endowed chairs, only a smattering of doctoral students, and two dedicated office workers who sorted the mail and ran off photocopies.

Curled up on a sectional cube, flipping idly through *Music Education for the Developmentally Disabled: Toward a Holistic Model*, was my colleague Isabelle Sumter, developer of an ingenious system of programmed tones said to stimulate dormant areas of damaged brain tissue and to awaken neural pathways. Clever experiments with rats (carried out in tandem with department scientists from none other than the Fenster Wing, courtesy of a generous grant from the Neural Sciences Foundation) had proven conclusively that listening to melodious intervals – thirds, sixths, octaves – increased the rats' ability to navigate through mazes and to find the hunk of cheese. Rats who listened to unrelenting noise showed no similar gains.

"Hi Luther."

"Hello, Isabelle." Isabelle had a lazy eye. I had difficulty maintaining eye contact, not knowing which one to focus upon.

"What do you think of this?" she asked. She carried around an electronic keyboard for when inspiration struck.

"Why, I feel the neurons sprouting this very minute," I said, riffling through *Ars Cantus Mensurabilis*, a 13th century treatise on musical notation.

"I'm trying to figure out what kinds of musical patterns the developmentally challenged respond to—"

"I really can't say, Isabelle. It's all excruciating to my ear," I offered by way of explanation. Certainly *I* was not ideally suited to adjudge the musicality of passages founded on the artificial intervals of our modern system of tuning.

She (or the one eye) stared at me venomously. "This is important work," she huffed. She was implementing a pilot program in the special education departments of six specially selected public schools, a program in which the captive student audience would be subjected to a smorgasbord of classical tunes and thereafter tested on critical abilities – *Does Jack first wake up? Does Jack first eat his breakfast? Determine the sequence of events* – to assess whether the music had succeeded in stimulating any neural networks.

"I don't doubt it," I said.

"Well, if you want to participate, let me know," she said. "I need music instructors who can liase with the special ed teachers."

"I will take it under advisement," I replied, filing it in my mental trash bin.

Isabelle – she who wandered around the faculty lounge, trying to determine the tonal sequences that would best stimulate the minds of laboratory animals with ablated prefrontal cortices and children who scored in the lowest percentiles of the Stanford-Binet intelligence test – was the recipient of the university's largesse. Yet *I*, a scholar of the earliest sources of music, the only one who appreciated what Pythagoras had discovered in his experiments on the gut-string lyre, the only one with a passing familiarity with the *Ars cantus mensurabilis* – had been relegated to the Fenster Wing, amid excrement-splattered animal cages. It was a sad commentary on the state of music. The darkest era since Rameau had handed out his leaflets decrying the irregular temperaments, since Pope John XII had banned polyphony out of a misguided notion that music could incite the population to ungodly acts, since William Braid White had "modernized" tuning with his odious system of cents.

I finished my crumb cake, bid *adieu* to Isabelle, and wandered into the department office. After removing the usual gunk from my mail box, flyers advertising the musical appearances of mediocre student bands, Burt's inspirational messages to the faculty (*Group piano can be fun! Erupt into a boogie…*), I found a letter, on heavy parchment paper, from one of my colleagues in the field of early music, Professor Ernst of the University of Hamburg. I ripped open the seal.

Herr Colleague:

For many years, nearly twenty, I have made the journey to New York to convene with my colleagues in the Early Music movement, to engage in lively debates regarding temperament, to listen to lecture concerning the Pythagorean proportions, to discuss the prevalence of Silbermann's six-comma meantone, to witness demonstrations of the mesolabium, etc.

I have endured trans-Atlantic flights in coach class with an awkward lute case. I have suffered the diatribes of Jacques St. Jacques, who cannot see beyond the Just intervals. I have defended myself against the slurs of Otto Schlanger (Traitor! Look at the bulbous nose and pitiable breeches!), who maintains that I have made a pact with the Devil. You cannot be a champion of medieval music while advocating for the ascendance of the equal temperament! He has shouted at me, with shaken fist. He defaced my lute case, my prized custom-made case, with juvenile pentagrams and cartoon renderings of bloated imps, a veritable Hieronymus Bosch of leering Devils and maimed corpses and plague-ridden cities. I have slept in faculty housing with Schlanger, who, like a medieval mendicant, refuses to bathe, revels in filth, and enjoys the perfume of his hairy armpit. During the last symposium he dragged me to an accursed "microbrewery" in Brooklyn, landing me in a vagrant's hospital with alcohol poisoning. He insisted that I accompany him to the tattoo parlor on St. Mark's Place, reciting Latinate liturgical verse while he howled in pain as a pair of colorful buxom mermaids was inked on his flaccid bicep.

I can no longer ask my university to fund this "wustrel[sic]" journey. I cannot room with Professor Schlanger, who bores me with his theorems and his strings of imaginary numbers, his "misgidded [sic]" belief that the Just intervals are embedded in the design of the universe itself.

I urge you and my fellow colleagues to embrace the equal temperament. It is but the inevitable evolution of centuries' worth of plainchant and obstinate instrument design that did not allow for modulation. What the Chinese had intuited in their experiments with bamboo pipes has been accomplished by splitting the octave into twelve equidistant steps, obliterating forever the useless distinctions between sharps and flats and enabling the orchestra to communicate in a lingua franca. Stop obsessing over diurnal commas and augmented fourths. We live in a modern world, my friend, an equal-tempered world (and have been, my friend, since Bach initiated the modern era with The Well-Tempered Clavier).

In my absence, it falls to you to prevent Schlanger from getting another ill-advised piercing or from wandering into a basement tattoo parlor.

17.

Ms. La Planta forwarded me a copy of Seven Happiness' answer to my verified complaint. In numbered paragraphs, it denied the allegations of the complaint, or denied knowledge of information sufficient to form a belief about the allegations of the complaint, and dared to assert a counterclaim against me for defamation and interference with business relations arising from my alleged "badmouthing" of the restaurant.

Infuriated, I called Ms. La Planta, who seemed unconcerned by the denials and the spurious counterclaim. "It's just legalise," she assured me, despite the fact that Seven Happiness denied knowledge of the incident, of Mother's demise, of having delivered wonton soup to the premises, wherein the fatal gelatinous agent of death resided. To wit:

¶ Seven Happiness, Inc., Seven Happiness LLC, and Bernice Wong, individually, were careless, negligent and failed to exercise ordinary care when, on or about July 23, 2015, they prepared, served and/or delivered to decedent, Celeste van der Loon, and/or her agent, Luther van der Loon, a plastic container of wonton soup, which, upon information and belief, was inadequately cooked and/or impermissibly allowed to cool, causing the wontons therein to harden, resulting in the death of decedent, Celeste van der Loon.

Denied.

¶ Seven Happiness, Inc., Seven Happiness LLC, and Bernice Wong, individually, were careless, negligent and failed to exercise ordinary care when, on or about July 23, 2015, they failed to warn decedent, Celeste van der Loon, of the dangers lurking in the murky broth, to wit, the known tendency of lye paste, particularly lye paste folded in the so-called Shanghai style, to become chewy, gummy and impossible to masticate; of the known danger presented by large leafs of bok choy; of the exponential danger presented by wontons and bok choy in tandem, particularly when obscured, in whole or in part, by murky broth.

Denied.

¶ Seven Happiness, Inc., Seven Happiness LLC, and Bernice Wong, individually, consciously chose to disregard a known risk when, on or about July 23, 2015, they defrosted a batch of wontons, on information and belief lot number 47921, purchased from a vendor on Mott Street known to engage in unsafe food practices, when, in further disregard of said known risk, they allowed the wontons to rapidly cool and to become chewy, owing to a shortage of deliverymen during peak delivery hours, that despite these enumerated risks, Seven Happiness nonetheless delivered to decedent Celeste van der Loon, at or about July 23, 2015, a steaming container of wonton soup, failing to apprise her of the dangers lurking within.

Denied.

¶ Seven Happiness, Inc., Seven Happiness LLC, and Bernice Wong, individually, intended to, and indeed, inflicted emotional distress on decedent's son, Luther van der Loon when, on or about July 23, 2015, he witnessed his mother, decedent Celeste van der Loon, experience foreign body airway obstruction ("FBAO") occasioned by the fatal plug, to wit, gasping, wheezing, turning blue, suffering for an estimated ten minutes while Luther van der Loon attempted to perform the Heimlich maneuver, recommended method for counteracting FBAO, as depicted in a poster prominently affixed to the wall of Seven Happiness take-out, to no avail.

Denied.

¶ That as a result of the foregoing, Luther van der Loon is bereft, adrift, experiencing what in the bereavement literature is described as *traumatic reactive bereavement*; he is paralyzed, unable to go on without his mother, to fathom life without her, to conceive of a world in which she is no longer present.

Denied.

The borough of Queens is the land of the dead. Tracts of burial ground extending for miles on either side of the Long Island Expressway; the final resting place for almost everyone expiring within the five-borough area. The cemetery in which Mother is buried lies within the shadow of "tanks" that belch fumes upon the deceased and mar their final rest with putrid exhalations. I suppose the ZAFT Corp. thought the dead were in no position to complain when they decided to build their electrical generating plant upon the border of the cemetery.

Older monuments are baroque, marble paeans to those no longer of this realm. Interspersed are smaller plots, auctioned off to those who could afford little more than a bronze plaque in the ground surrounded by crab grass. Mother, back in the 1970s, had invested in a small mausoleum. It lacked the dramatic angels or weeping Madonnas of some of the more ornate mausoleums, but at least afforded a private space for my suffering.

I knelt on the velvet padded pew, under the stained-glass window of a crucified Jesus. What awaited all of us? A host of heavenly saints, a glorified body, reunion with all who had pre-deceased us? Or invidious decomposition, beginning with our last exhalation and ceasing when the multitudinous bacteria to which we were host succeeded in eating us from the inside out, in a process quaintly known as *putrefaction*? The body ceases to be, but the spirit does not, people had assured me as they clutched my hand in M. & Sons Funeraral Chapel. *The body is but a shell*, said Cecilia, who was raised a Roman Catholic but whose belief system incorporated Jungian animism and the reincarnation dogma of Hindus and Buddhists.

What would I find if I took a chisel to the mausoleum wall, and pried open the coffin where Mother was laid to rest? These thoughts were so overpowering at times that I found myself pounding against the wall of the mausoleum, expecting an answer from the Beyond.

When I was a child, Mother and I used to chase butterflies. We trapped monarchs, brown elfins and Eastern-tail blues in jars, taking them home and allowing them to flutter, free, in the steamy bathroom, our indoor sanctuary (steam necessary to open up my gunked-up sinuses). When they died, at the end of their life cycle, Mother helped me pin their wings to cardboard backing, and press them inside glass, forever ours, to gaze upon their iridescent wings.

After Father had been gone several months on a "business trip," Mother suggested a special butterfly hunt and horticultural diversion on the Greens. It was spring and the flowers just blooming; the wind trilled in E-flat. Mother pointed out a male Eastern-tail blue, perched on a branch, and I caught him on the first swoop. Usually, I skulked after a specimen for an eternity, cursing the awkward gait and perennial sniffling that made sneaking up on anything, let alone a winged creature, all but impossible. "I caught him, Mother!" I remembered shouting. The thrill of the moment still permeates me; the smell of cherry blossoms suffuses the air. She hastened over with the jar and nudged him in, swiftly screwing the top on. "There," she said, smiling at me, brushing a lock from my Cro-Magnon forehead (I must have inherited my looming brow from Father, for Mother's brow was high and perfectly sculpted), offering me a *petit-four*. The taste of bittersweet chocolate was still on my tongue when she said, "Luther, I have no reason to think your father is coming back." The wings flapping desperately in the jar. A disjointed rhythm, one-TWO, emphasis on the off-beat. "Did you hear me, sweetheart?" The Eastern-tail blue, trapped in the jar. It was the last time I would ever breathe joy untempered by misery, the last time I would experience bliss without tonal dissonance. (I would soon develop a skin condition whose outbreaks coincided with stress and hormonal fluctuations, my emotions inside-out, leaving me no choice but to dress in long-sleeve shirts with high collars.) "You'll always have me," she said, pulling me closer.

The harpsichord is a dynamically-limited instrument, resting inside a fragile case.

Oh, Mother! She was no longer here to mute my sadnesses, to act as a damper on my emotions, to comment on the new arrangement I had worked out for *Byrd one brere*, to wipe the drivel from my nose, to apply salve to my accursed eczema, to sing *Trinklieder* in two-part harmony, to declaim the parts of the Roman de Fauvel, to hold forth on Wagner's theory of *Gesamtkunstwerk* – music is the only art form that promises transcendence, the only art form that approaches the divine (put aside the fact that Wagner was a heretic, an atheist, and a foul-mouthed aesthete).

I rose from the kneeler, dusted off my knees, and locked the door to the mausoleum behind me.

18.

In class the following week, I demonstrated, by means of tuning forks, the precise difference in frequency between the perfect Pythagorean intervals and their counterparts in the equal temperament. The acoustically pure fifth, at 701.96 cents, does not deviate significantly from the equal tempered fifth at 700 cents. However, there is a gross discrepancy between the acoustically pure third, at 386.31 cents, and the equal tempered third, at 400 cents.

How is it, I wondered, that we have become accustomed to this gaping interval? And why does no one care?

When intervals deviate from the perfect proportions, their overtones "beat," or audibly clash. Even William, my least inspired student, was able to apprehend this phenomenon. (We were now three in number. The coloratura soprano had dropped the course, fearing the effects of inhaled animal excrement upon her delicate vocal cords, and the composition major had withdrawn, citing ethical objections to "senseless" animal experimentation; he, apparently, had divulged the location of the concealed gray door to the protestors, necessitating the posting of a sentry in the hallway to prevent demonstrations and animal rights "terrorism," the uncaging of lobotomized chimps and fattened rats who had been electrocuted for seeking rewards.)

"That doesn't sound right," William said, referring to the equal-tempered third.

"This so-called 'sonority' is the fundament of our modern musical world. Our notion of tonality. And yet hear how much it deviates from the pure interval." I held the tuning fork aloft.

Triumph, however, was short-lived. We were forced to evacuate based on a threat from the Animal Liberation Organization to firebomb the chimpanzee lab. The gray door blocked by protestors, we were forced, one by one, to jump through a third-story window onto inflatable mats that had been set up by campus security forces.

Free the chimps now! Free the chimps now! they shouted. *Chimp killer! Chimp killer!* Undergraduates with piercings and pustulent eruptions (easily eradicated by the very same products they were boycotting for animal testing) shook their fists at us, evidently confusing us with the laboratory scientists who were cowering somewhere in the subbasement.

"What do you have to say for yourself?" their ringleader demanded. He thrust a photo of a chimpanzee that was immobilized in a vise under my nose.

"I'm afraid there's been a misunderstanding," I replied, pushing my way through, shielding my face from photographers who would tag me as the enemy, upload my image to the website of the Animal Liberation Organization (www.freelabrat.com), encourage the university to choke me of funding.

Meet me at the Hairy Monk, I mouthed to my students. *I have a rescue cat*, I lied to the protestors. I led the mob to believe I was the kind who patronized animal shelters, looking for the most pitiable, the most abused and emaciated pet to take in, to nurture and responsibly neuter or spay.

I eventually made it across the shoal of Broadway and onto St. Mark's Place. I stopped and looked around to ensure that no protestors had followed me. None had. My head echoed with cries of *Chimp killer! Liberate the animals!*

The Hairy Monk was located midblock, between a head shop and a tattoo parlor. *Drink and be Merry*, a sign of a rotund friar beckoned. My students had reserved a table and ordered a pitcher of beer. I sat down, still shaken. "Do you know what they do to the chimps when the experiment is done? They hack them up! They slice their brains like deli meat!" Frankie declared, before consoling herself with a chicken wing in buffalo sauce.

William, a founding member of the band Death Trapp, likened the experience of being mobbed by animal activists to diving into the mosh pit. "You don't know what will happen. You just get carried along. Sometimes they just want to touch you. Sometimes they rip your clothes off. Do you want to play darts?" he proposed.

I refrained, citing extreme nearsightedness occasioned by communing with illuminated manuscripts under the dimmest of lighting conditions.

"So, what do you do when you're not teaching? Do you play one of those pipe organs or something?" William inquired.

"I play in period music ensembles," I replied. Infrequent, intimate *soirées* at the homes of wealthy benefactors, the occasional Renaissance fair, and, of course, the Early Music Symposium (projected attendance: thirty-five).

"Can you make enough dough?" he asked, divining the evident precariousness of my financial arrangements.

"I lead a comfortable, if not extravagant, lifestyle," I said, my salary augmented by a modest inheritance and appearance fees guaranteed by the popularity of the Renaissance fair.

"I'm just, you know, struggling right now. If my band doesn't make it, I don't know how much longer I can scrape by," he lamented, the eternal plaint of the musician, always on the verge of penury and subject to the whims of his patron (whether it be the Pope, King Ludwig II of Bavaria, or his record producer, clamoring for a hit).

"I mean, I'm so sick of these side gigs. Kinko's fired me because I, uh, don't look corporate," he said, presumably referring to his long blonde dreadlocks and harlequin makeup. "Now I work at Tiki Burger, midnight shift. No one cares what I look like since I'm in the kitchen. Gotta wear this hairnet, though. Health department bullshit. But I need this job. Can't survive otherwise. My bud Wes, the drummer, knows someone who knows someone at the Bitter End, but I don't know if that's gonna lead anywhere," he sighed.

I had wandered, once or twice, into the local Tiki Burger, a chain store peddling an array of specialty burgers, including Polynesian Paradise (with pineapple slices and grilled ham), and the Kung Pao (glazed with soy sauce and chili paste). I had tried to order from the menu, *The burger combo, fries please?*, but was overcome with dread, a sinking feeling, finding myself as limp as the blue stick figure in the poster for *How to render aid to a choking victim.* Would anyone help me if I were stricken, slumped on the floor, a lettuce leaf stuck in my throat? Would anyone care?

"Anyway, I just don't know how long I can flip burgers, you know?"

I did know. It was Mother's largesse, and only Mother's largesse, that had enabled me to attend our esteemed university, to pursue doctoral studies over eight long years, to devote myself to medieval and Renaissance musical scholarship, concentrating on pre-mensural practices during the Ars Nova. It was Mother who encouraged me to apply for a post-doctoral fellowship and to journey to the Continent; Mother who paid the pitiable sum for my lodgings in the monastery so I could commune with the Wolfenbüttel Codex and other brittle sources of Notre Dame polyphony. Her son was now, thanks to a diabolical department head, languishing in an annex devoted to animal experimentation, a place where no natural light penetrated and the lights were always on – part of an experiment, apparently, to foul up the animals' circadian rhythms.

"Have you thought of busking?" I asked. The time-honored tradition of the impoverished musician. Once we wandered the streets of Genoa or Venice, serenading the medieval populace; now we opened our guitar cases in Washington Square Park, begging for spare change, an e-mail to add to our fan list, an impulse purchase of our self-produced CD.

"*Draw and Quarter U* doesn't go over well with the afternoon lunch crowd," replied William.

"Perhaps the dive bars of the East Village?" I suggested.

"We're trying. But it's hard even to get an unpaid gig," William mumbled, barely intelligible, particularly with *Free Bird* blaring in the background (some things never changed, least of all rock bands' odes to former band members killed prematurely in small plane accidents). The Renaissance had its share of forgettable tunes, madrigals and *chansons* that struck a passing fancy, only to be relegated to the dustbin of musical history, unworthy of analysis. The bulk of history is filled with misbegotten attempts, cliché-ridden melodies, tunes not worth remembering.

"Should all else fail," I brightened, "Professor Sumter is looking for help implementing music programs for the developmentally challenged."

Dear Prof. Ernst:

I am in receipt of your missive postmarked Hiddensee. I trust from the stamp that you are enjoying a seaside holiday in the Baltics — you have always recommended same to me as promising relief from sinus congestion and infernal allergies. I am rubbing my eyes as we speak. Though the trees are almost bare, winter upon us, enough spores are in the air apparently to drive the air quality index into the high upper ranges.

I take issue with your statement that I "obsess" over diurnal commas. At what point does the desirability of uniformity and simplicity in tuning justify the trampling of hundreds of years of musical tradition, formulas derived thousands of years ago by Pythagoras as evidence of the internal harmonies of the universe?

I am of course greatly saddened by your decision not to attend this year's Early Music Symposium. Enjoy your salt bath.

19.

Cecilia was ever cognizant of the stages of grief. Depression, or despair, the problematic fourth stage.

"We're not staying here during the holidays," Cecilia announced. "I don't think it's a good idea." We would not be eating the Christmas ham upon Mother's china, exchanging gifts in the salon, singing a lugubrious *God Rest Ye Merry Gentlemen*, reminding me of what I had indubitably, irreparably lost.

"What about Aveline?" I protested. Without regular practice, arthritis seized my long digits, warping the fourth metacarpal.

"You can manage," Cecilia said. "I'll massage your joints." Cecilia had taken courses in healing massage, an art that posited that stress and life traumas could be liberated from the body through selective pressure points.

"But where will we go?" I protested. My parents were specters. Hers, though very much alive, residents of Saratoga Springs, N.Y., disapproved of our relationship and resented the fact that I had never married Cecilia. The last time we paid them a visit, five years ago, I lambasted her parents' musical preferences (the Boston Pops), and was made to eat my turkey leg alone, out-of-doors, with nary a glove to protect my delicate digits. There was nothing for us in the Victorian cottage of Mr. and Mrs. Wesley Crocker, with its out-of-tune *piano-forte* and stale biscuits.

"Well, I've given it some thought." She sat in the bishop's chair, *Mother's* bishop's chair, and dug into a Styrofoam "cup o' soup," chicken bits and reheatable, limp noodles. She informed me that she had considered, and rejected, a tropical clime (lack of snow and festive wintry atmosphere). She had next considered, and rejected, Bavaria, Mother's birthland (too "emotionally charged" and "stressful" during my period of mourning, a place where I could not help but brood about Mother as I lingered in the *Festspielhaus* and obsessed over finding an intact Baroque church organ that had not been destroyed by bombers during World War II). Finally, she settled on a charming bed & breakfast in a small town in the eastern provinces of Québec, a place where we could forge a new Christmas tradition, free of Mother's ghost and the obligation to cook the Christmas ham. We would arrive a few days early to help me "acclimate."

"You can practice your French, Luther," she said, slurping up the last noodle.

"My 'French,' as you call it, is limited to an understanding of fourteenth-century archaic French and certainly does not encompass the *Franglais* spoken by our northern neighbors," I replied.

"It'll be fine. I think it will be a healing experience," Cecilia said, manipulating the tender arc of my rotator cuff, one of the areas of the body in which I harbored stress and unexpelled grief.

"Very well," I acquiesced.

We drove six hours through upstate New York and Vermont, pausing only to refill the gas tank and to avail ourselves of the "amenities" of the Walt Whitman rest stop. My sensitive stomach could not handle the dubious beef of a chain burger, nor its limp lettuce, its special sauces, its odious slice of American "cheese," a synthesized product bearing no resemblance to its namesake. I sat glumly at a picnic table, parka drawn tightly around my neck, while Cecilia ate a Whopper Jr., splattering map of North America with juices from same.

"Why don't you eat something?" she begged me, worried that I would be famished upon arrival.

"I'm fine," I assured her.

Cecilia wiped her hands on a napkin and off we were. At twilight, we arrived at the Vermont-Québec border. Perhaps "border" is overstating things: we were unceremoniously informed, at the end of the street, that we were leaving the United States of America and arriving in Canada. I almost missed the sign, buried as it was in a grove of fir trees.

The Québécois are the only fitting rivals I've ever seen, in matters of Christmas decoration, to the residents of the outer boroughs of New York City. There were giant inflatable snow globes, miniature worlds in empty air and polyurethane. Electrified scenes of old villages and carolers. The *bon homme de neige* in scarf, top hat and stony eyes. Santa Claus and his full retinue could be seen landing on rooftops, Rudolph's nose flickering in the darkness. It was like being in a wax museum, or a polyvinyl museum, of Christmas. Remarking upon one garish *bon homme de neige*, Cecilia missed the turn-off and ran into an embankment. It took a moment for the hilarity to subside, to be replaced by a feeling of real terror, or panic, the natural urge Cecilia called the *fight or flight mechanism*, survival or death, as simple as that. Since Mother's passing, I'd become resigned to my own inevitable demise, no longer thinking it a far-off prospect.

I pushed open the door and escaped onto the roof. Cecilia's door had jammed and she was obliged to follow me. I'm sure she rued the Whopper Jr. as she squeezed through. By the time the roadside authorities arrived it was well after midnight, our breath frozen.

"Mother, where are you?" I shouted inwardly, looking upon the silent, lit-up boulevards of Santa Clauses, the backlit manger scenes, the empty crèches.

Here and there a colored bulb had blown out. Snow globes tumbled in the wind. Stars glimmered somewhere above.

"Ich bin hier," *I am here*, I said, not expecting a response.

The bed-and-breakfast was charming enough: an old Victorian, canary yellow, with a wide front porch. Our proprietor, Micheline, was a young widow who occupied the first floor. She welcomed us, in roughly-accented English, with a *bûche de Noël* – a layered holiday cake in the shape of a meat loaf.

The next morning, she made *creton*, "typical" Québécois fare – something fatty, unintelligible, that I was to smear upon my breakfast toast.

"Thank you," Cecilia said, ever respectful of other people and their customs. I would have preferred marmalade or a slab of butter. "If you don't mind me asking," she said, "how long have you been a widow?"

"Three years, this Noel," she replied. "*Crise de cardiaque,*" she said, for which we needed no translation. She pointed to the chair in which I was sitting. "There," she said, "*il s'est évanoui.*"

Her husband had suffered a sudden cardiac event while seated in the very same chair in which I was struggling to get an even layer of *creton* on my stale baguette. Upon hearing that I was a musician, Micheline insisted that I play something upon the switch-activated instrument she called an organ. It had programmed beats such as "bossa nova," "samba," and "polka," that could be activated with a flick of a switch.

I tried to explain that I was a professor of medieval and Renaissance music, that unless she wanted to hear something by Gillaume de Machaut or Josquin du Pres, an Agnus Dei in four parts, she would likely be disappointed. The phrase *professeur de musique*, however, incited her all the more. She waved some sheet music at me, keyboard transcriptions of Christmas classics that a person of even the most limited musical ability could sight read while maintaining a steady beat.

I regaled them with an improvised contrapuntal version of "Little Town of Bethlehem."

"Magnifique!" Micheline screeched.

Christmas morning we went to L'Eglise de Sacré Coeur, a stone edifice dating from the seventeenth century. Directly across the road was an Anglican version and just next door an Episcopalian one, leaving no shortage of places in which to celebrate our Savior's birth. "Joyeux Noël," I murmured in response to those who felt compelled to tell me the same. Mother and I were not regular churchgoers. She preferred the Episcopalian church around the block, reasoning that the liturgy was similar enough to that of the Roman Catholic church into which she had been baptized, refusing to get drawn into doctrinal differences about the papacy, the transfiguration, etc. I had lost respect for churches long ago, mainly because they had let their organ pipes be reconfigured in conformity with the equal temperament.

"Sacré Coeur" was no different. Was I the only one who could hear these malevolent dissonances, tones artificially split for tuning ease, to enable keyboard instruments to play alongside their less, fretted cousins, the lutes and guitarras? Micheline's voice, a warbling mezzo-soprano, careened heavenward. Cecilia sensibly had her psalm book shut. Even if she could somehow manage the French pronunciations, she was tone-deaf.

"Amen," the chorale leader sang with an odious melisma.

We exited in orderly fashion, passing the life-size crèche on the lawn. Baby Jesus' halo flickered courtesy of an elaborate electrical setup. The star of Bethlehem was suspended high above, probably rigged from one of the flying buttresses.

"Incroyable," gushed Micheline.

After mass, Micheline went caroling with several friends. Cecilia and I returned to our charming Victorian, where I politely suggested that she read or drink eggnog so I could have time to myself.

"It's Christmas," she said, she of pantheistic leanings and a psychologist's disdain for the hereafter, though she thoroughly respected each client's "belief systems" regarding same.

"What do you care?" I scoffed. "It's just a pagan ritual re-enacted in Christian form, right? The Star from the East, the offerings of the wise men."

"What matters is that it's important to you and figures in your belief system," she said, the infernal "echoing" of the trained psychotherapist, mirroring statements in an endless verbal labyrinth.

"I just need some time." I turned and went upstairs, first removing my boots per the "house rules" Micheline had posted next to the stairwell. (Please do not remove more than one book from library at a time; put all board games in the *placard*; do not make coffee before 6 a.m. or after 10:00 p.m., the coffee machine grumbles.) Our double room was pleasant, with a handmade quilt, a sunny window, an antique washbasin, and a mirrored bureau in which my sorry self was reflected. I lay on the brass bed, hands behind my head, and stared out the window. Snow blanketed the ground, white as far as I could see. I imagined a similar scene in Bavaria, mother's Alpine homeland, though I had never been. Icicles dripping from the eaves of chalets; intrepid souls cross-country skiing through the town, hauling firewood. We had always meant to go, to visit the handful of distant relations she called cousins, to attend mass at the Baroque church she assured me still had an organ tuned in the quarter comma mean-tone, though I suspected it was tuned in a variant of Silbermann's one-sixth comma, often erroneously referred to as "mean-tone."

"Should we exchange presents now?" Cecilia stood in the door frame, intent on making me reenact the traditional Christmas rituals. She had a lumpy package, containing a hand-knit sweater, something professorial, even though I was lecturing to a handful of students in a building consecrated to animal experimentation. The other package (silver wrapped) contained a bottle of single malt Scotch.

"Thank you, thank you so much," I murmured. I removed Cecilia's packages from my luggage, a first edition of *Man and His Symbols*, the plates still in rather good condition, as well as a Berber necklace I had picked up on St. Mark's Place, knowing Cecilia to be enamored of ethnic jewelry, especially clunky pieces to go with her flowing, brightly-colored dresses.

"Thank you," she gushed, "I really wasn't expecting any-thing."

"You're welcome," I said.

"Should we say a prayer of remembrance?" she asked, clap-ping her hands. "Purely nondenominational."

"I'd rather not," I replied. I wanted no prayer of remem-brance, no masses said in the deceased's honor, no rosaries by nuns in the Spanish highlands. I did not want to acknowledge that Mother was no longer here, that I had no one with whom to eat marzipan or to sip tea, on cracked blue saucers.

"All right." Cecilia looked crestfallen. I was proving resil-ient to most of the methods that had worked on her grieving clientele, those for whom a prayer for the departed, a poem for the bereaved, a reflection on the inevitable cycle of life, worked quite well.

She went downstairs. I remained in our room, pondering geometrical and mechanical solutions to the splitting of the octave. The problem had proven insoluble using Euclidian geometry. Francisco Salinas, in the sixteenth century, suggested use of the mesolabium, a mathematical instrument for finding two mean proportions. Yet the solution was never satisfactory: in splitting the scale equidistantly, in the manner first suggested by Prince Chu Tsai-Yu, in his treatise *A New Account of the Science of Pitch Pipes*, the tonalities of scale and key had forever been altered.

Micheline returned midafternoon. I heard her bustling in the kitchen for an hour or two, listening to the Boston Pops or other infernal "classical" ensemble. At the first bars of Vivaldi's "Spring," I slammed the door, not so discreetly.

"*Dîner*," Micheline announced, summoning us to the table. She had prepared a traditional English supper, roast beef with fingerling potatoes, as well as Québécois fare, goose in an *emballage* of pastry dough. It was a lot of food for only three, but Micheline said they liked to prepare food for the "guests who were no longer at the table," that is to say, the hungry, disembodied spirits of those who were no longer among us.

"Charming," I said.

"My husband liked very much this meal. His parents were Scotch and followed many highland traditions. They did not like pâté, or mousses, but they were fond of head cheese. I like to make this supper in memory of him," she said, a tear appearing in her eye. "Your wife," she nodded at Cecilia, making the assumption most did, "has been helping me process (emphasis on the second syllable) this experience of death. It has been three years, and still, I expect him to be here," she said, pointing to the seat I was occupying.

"Does it bother you that he's sitting in that chair?" Cecilia asked. "It's okay. These associations are normal. He can move someplace else," she said, elbowing me, forcing me to move to an uncomfortable Victorian cane-backed chair. Cecilia gave me a look imploring me *to share*. I refused to be drawn into this impromptu group therapy, this circle of grieving. I turned away and carved up the roast beef. Why was it better to share one's feelings, to engage in a group cry?

"Luther's had a recent loss," Cecilia informed Micheline, solidifying the fact of Mother's disappearance, for which I truly resented her.

"Oh, really," Micheline said, the flat "r" giving her difficulty.

"Yes," I said, handing her a platter. "My mother." It was the first time I had acknowledged the loss publicly, other than in the thirty-page complaint I had filed seeking damages from Seven Happiness restaurant for the deprivation of my mother and the loss of her services.

"The mother is difficult," Micheline commiserated.

Cecilia nodded, reinforcing Micheline's statements and unfortunately encouraging her to unburden more. "It was a terrible scene, really. He was eating at this very table," she said, pointing at the seat I had just vacated. "He was eating this same meal – I don't know why I continue to make this."

"It's a way of reliving his final moments, of recreating this final time with him," Cecilia interjected. "It's totally normal."

"Yes, well he was eating this roast beef, or maybe this potato. He looked at me, lovingly, as if to express gratitude for the meal."

"Isn't that a lovely moment, Micheline? Something to visualize," Cecilia coached.

"Suddenly, his expression changed. The color drained. He was pale, pale, almost blue."

"Cyanosis," I coughed into a napkin.

"He collapsed on the floor. I tried to do this – how do you say it? – mouth-to-mouth, but he was limp, nothing." She started crying. "And there is no ambulance service here," she said. "The hospital is thirty minutes away. No, no," she searched for the word.

"Defibrillator?" I offered. Cecilia scowled at me.

"Yes, none of this."

"There was no pulse, nothing," she wept.

I glared at Cecilia. If she could not force me to attend sessions with her colleague, the esteemed Dr. Fein, if she could not make me rehash the fatal incident in all its ignominious detail – the first phase, acute airway obstruction; the second phase, rapid, deep inhalation, driving the foreign body ("FB") deeper into the larynx; the final phase, laryngospasm – I paraphrase loosely from the autopsy report – then she could make me suffer through Micheline's fatal reminiscences.

"Would you like dessert?" Micheline asked. She returned with a tray of freshly-brewed coffee, the *bûche de Noël,* and a bowl of rice pudding.

The mood had grown somber. I stirred my coffee, lost in thought. Micheline asked if I wouldn't mind performing another carol. She flicked a switch to warm up the organ. Cecilia curled up on the sofa. I retrieved the book of carols from its place under the bench. Perhaps a few bars of "Jingle Bells" to lift the mood. The keys on the organ were so easily depressed that even an arthritic grandmother would sound heavy-handed. Not like Aveline, who required a deft touch and a crisp attack.

"*Sapin vert, sapin vert,*" Micheline substituted for "Jingle Bells," and I went along with it, because it rhymed and I wasn't interested in a literal translation. I indulged requests for "God Bless Ye Merry Gentlemen," and "Deck the Halls," before an exaggerated yawn and a false claim of being tired.

"Joyeux Noël," Micheline said, waving goodnight as we ascended the creaky stairs. I turned in and pretended to be asleep, while Cecilia stayed up to the early hours of the morning, reading Jung by the light of a gas lamp.

We left the following morning, one day earlier than anticipated. I was not interested in a scenic drive of the Christmas displays. Nor in ice skating, or a Boxing Day dinner at the inn on the lake. Cecilia seemed disappointed, evidently because I was still having difficulty enjoying everyday life, a sign of persistent grief, or depression, or both. I told her that I'd merely had enough of Micheline and her lonely cheer, and was ready to get back home to my new semester's lesson plan, arrangements for the Early Music Symposium, rehearsal for the faculty recital, in which I planned to play a version of "New York, New York, It's a Wonderful Town" in the mean-tone, just to infuriate Burt.

We drove the distance from Québec to New York City in under eight hours, stopping only once, just north of Albany, to relieve Cecilia's bladder. Cecilia suggested that we stop at the cemetery en route; I demurred, even though it was not yet "closing time," wanting to keep my grief in a separate sphere, where only I could wallow in it. We continued along the Cross-Bronx Expressway, bypassing Queens, the land of the dead, with its acres of chiseled memorials and weathered stone angels. "I'll see you another day, Mother," I assured her, when I could refresh the flowers in the marble vault and weep privately upon the altar.

When we got home, laden with weekend bags and the infamous *bûche de Noël* (which Micheline had insisted we take home), the doorman slipped me a note. It was from Ms. La Planta, asking to schedule an informal meeting, stating that she had questions about the "incident" and "resuscitation."

"Who's that from?" Cecilia asked, ever inquisitive.

"Just a Christmas note from one of the neighbors."

"Nice of them to remember you during the holidays," she remarked.

We settled ourselves in the apartment. After I had inspected Aveline to ensure that she had not suffered any untoward vibration or unexpected humidity during our absence, I locked myself in the bedroom and called my counselor-at-law.

"What's this about?" I asked.

"Some questions have come up about the circumstances of your mother's death – I'm just trying to anticipate their defenses."

"Questions, like what?"

"Well, they've seized upon a finding in the autopsy report that your mother's dentition left less to be desired."

"What does that mean?" I asked, exasperated.

"Well, people with bad teeth are not able to chew as well and more likely to choke on foreign bodies."

"Are you saying she choked because she couldn't chew the wonton? Is that what you're saying?"

"I'm not saying anything. I'm just trying to anticipate their defenses. Do you have her dental records? Or even the name of her dentist? I need to obtain the records from the doctor so I know what we're dealing with."

"Fine, fine," I replied. "Dr. Wong-Goldman, on Madison Avenue." We had an annual appointment, booked together, which I realized was scheduled for next month. I didn't know whether I should cancel our joint appointment, or just show up and explain that Mother had passed, the victim of "FBAO"

– foreign body airway obstruction, unnervingly pronounced by Ms. La Planta as if it were a word unto itself. F-BOW. I had always held Dr. Wong-Goldman, D.D.S., in the highest esteem – she was unrelenting with the pick – but now I wondered whether she had been doing her job.

"I have some other questions," Ms. La Planta continued. "Did your mother drink?"

"Do you mean was she an alcoholic?"

"Yes, in a nutshell."

"No, she did not drink to excess," I said, exclusive of Bavaria nights at Rolf's Biergarten, information I withheld as not pertinent.

"Because the other side is going to try to show that her reflexes were slowed, whether due to age, or alcohol or drug use."

"Drug use?"

"Well, if she were taking sleeping pills, anti-anxiety medications, anything like that, it might affect her reflexes. Gag reflex, swallowing reflex."

I audibly inhaled. I didn't take well to this inquisition of mother, this post-mortem on the condition of her teeth and inclination toward drink or prescription pharmaceuticals. "Isn't this just unfairly attacking the victim? Isn't this slanderous?"

"Well, it goes to causation so unfortunately it's within limits. Strictly speaking, you can't slander the dead. The dead are not considered, legally, to have a reputation that can be tarnished."

Now I understood why Carlo Gesualdo had been assailed as a murderous cuckold and half-demon, why Machaut was reputed to have fathered scores of children out of wedlock, why Leonin was decried as a homosexual, sodomite and sexual deviant: there were no legal repercussions for insulting the dead. The dead have but limited legal recourse.

"There's one other thing," Ms. La Planta stated. "The other side is wondering whether you tried to revive the decedent."

"Why? What does that have to do with anything?"

"Resuscitation attempts are known, sometimes, to do more harm than good. To cause the FB to lodge further in the airway, out of reach."

"So I would be at fault for trying to save her? They want to avoid liability by saying my rescue efforts, not their wontons, were the cause of her death?" I tried to keep my voice down. Cecilia was in the other room, unpacking.

"Well, as I understand the sequence of events, you tried to expel the FB by performing the Heimlich maneuver."

"That is correct."

"Well, it shouldn't be a problem. It's just known to be inadvisable to perform what they call a 'blind sweep' of a choking victim's airway."

I drove my fist into her abdomen, trying to dislodge the blockage. When that failed, I started CPR, my puffs of oxygen, desperately administered, not reaching the lungs, carbon dioxide reaching critical levels, lips turning blue, like that of her favorite china.

"All right," she said, "I'll correct that misperception. But we need the dental records," she reminded me, hanging up.

20.

Tuesdays and Thursdays I held office hours from two to four o'clock. Burt let me retain an office in the Tishman Building, though I had otherwise been relegated to the Fenster Wing.

I had an hour remaining before I would be displaced by my office mate Marlene. She'd done her doctoral work on Dalcroze eurhythmics, a system of musical training that emphasized music's connection to other art forms. Emile-Jacques Dalcroze advocated the teaching of programmed dance movements, each corresponding to a rhythmic figure – for example, skipping to represent a dotted whole note. This method was supposed to imbue the music student with a natural sense of rhythm and musical structure.

Scrolling through my e-mail, I saw that Ernst had sent another malign missive.

Herr Colleague:

The margin notations on Haydn's Opus No. 77 prove the exact opposite of what you assert. The designation l'istesso tuono ("same tone") is a reminder to the player not to raise the D#. The notation is an unequivocal assertion by the composer that D# and E flat are in fact the same note and that the prevalent tuning system is in fact the equal temperament. Though muckrackers[sic] like you continue to insist that irregular temperaments were used well into the nineteenth century, the irrefutable evidence shows that from the Baroque onward the preference was for the equal temperament. The Well-Tempered Clavier is an equal-tempered clavier, not a shifting six-comma meantone. Have a nice day.

Dear Ernst,

I beg to differ. Where you see unequivocal evidence of the equal temperament ("l'istesso tuono") I see proof of a mean-tone variant. The direction to "play the same tone" indicates that D# and E-flat were in fact held to be separate pitches — not the same, inglorious note into which they were merged when the equal temperament abolished the diesis. Haydn, it is well known, advocated the adoption of the Charles Claggett forte-piano, a keyboard design consisting of thirty-nine tones to the octave (not twelve tones to the octave, the hideous compression wrought by the equal temperament).
QED.

I left my office at quarter to four. Snow had been cleared from the sidewalks by establishments eager to avoid liability for slipping accidents, forming embankments that were equally, if not more dangerous. Slush, mixed with grime, marred the path from corner to corner and made for an unpleasant walk home. I had counterpoint exercises to grade for the next class. The professor of Renaissance music, alas, had no teaching assistant upon whom to foist these thankless duties, no multiple choice test he could administer at semester's end, and be done with it, like his colleagues in the Departments of Psychology and Sociology. No, his work was labor intensive, and difficult, the work of master and apprentice, of feeble attempt and excruciating correction.

Cecilia greeted me at the door, an expression of concern on her face. "Luther, what's this?" she asked, holding up the frozen container of wonton soup. The fatal broth itself, frozen and preserved by me. First in some perverse remembrance, then in response to express direction from Ms. La Planta to preserve the agent of Mother's death so its choking potential could be evaluated in the laboratory.

"It's a container of wonton soup," I replied. I peered under the dust cover to ensure that Aveline had not suffered any untoward environmental disturbances during my absence.

"I can see that," she said. "Why is it in the freezer?"

I thought that a ham hock and the *bûche de Noël* had provided ample camouflage, but Cecilia had evidently run across it while rummaging in the frozen food.

"Please do not allow it to defrost." I took the container from her reverently and placed it back in the freezer. Ms. La Planta told me not to defrost and refreeze, lest the consistency of the wontons be compromised.

"Why are you keeping it?" she said. "It's morbid."

"Morbid? And re-making your dead husband's final meal every Christmas, serving it to guests sitting on the very same chair on which he suffered his *crise de cardiaque*, is not morbid, it's a 'healthy expression of grief?'" I parroted her words to the Québécoise.

"This is different. This is not merely part of the stage, or the scene of death, this is the very agent of your mother's death. It would be like Micheline keeping a clogged artery as a souvenir."

"I don't think your simile is apt," I said, returning the soup to the freezer and closing the door. "This was Mother's last meal, just like the infernal roast beef was Didier's."

"But it was not the roast beef that killed Didier," she said. "It was only incidental, a prop. This was the very same wonton soup your mother choked on. It's a perverse souvenir. It's like you want to exercise dominion over the thing that caused your mother's death. You want to freeze it, neutralize its destructive potential."

It went on like this. Cecilia scrutinizing my motives for holding on to the wonton soup; I maintaining a firm grip on the freezer door so as not to subject the soup to further fluctuations in temperature. I could not divulge that I was preserving the soup per the direction of my personal injury lawyer, Ms. La Planta, whom Cecilia believed capitalized on people's grief, leading them to believe that grief could be expunged by the expedient of a lawsuit against a deep pocket who could be said to have proximately caused their loss.

Ms. La Planta intended to demonstrate, by comparison to a non-fatal serving of the soup, that the wontons in the soup ingested by Mother were undercooked, gelatinous, difficult to masticate. She intended to show that Seven Happiness was a shoddy enterprise, guilty of negligence in food handling, by introducing evidence that its rating had been revised downward from a C+ to a C minus by the Department of Health.

But Cecilia was correct. Nothing would bring back Mother. Not obsessive playing of *Byrd one brere*, or browsing through *Bavaria – A Pictorial History*, open on the coffee table.

"I'm just trying to help you," Cecilia said, patting me on the hand.

"I know," I conceded. I allowed her to massage my spasming lower back. Her small, sturdy hands, while unsuited to the keyboard, excelled at breaking up the tension in my lumbosacral spine. "There," I said, encouraging her rigorous manipulations. "Much better."

21.

The following day, I received from Ms. La Planta helpful literature on "How to Prepare for Your Upcoming Deposition." It behooved me to listen carefully to the question asked, to answer only the question asked, and not to "volunteer" information, which would inexorably lead to trouble. Your lawyer will sit at your side throughout the deposition and will object to questions she deems inappropriate. Very rarely, she will direct you not to answer a question. DO NOT SPECULATE, the literature warned. If you do not know the answer to a question, simply say *I don't know*. If you cannot remember, simply say *I don't remember* or *I have no recollection*.

I scheduled an appointment at the offices of Bloodstone & Moore to help prepare for my deposition. I arrived at the scheduled hour with a sheaf of polyphony exercises under my arm, in the event my attorneys were detained at court or counseling someone else who had been grievously injured. The firm newsletter, sitting on a glass table in the waiting room, indicated that the firm had been instrumental in obtaining a settlement on behalf of children poisoned by lead paint in housing projects, part of their commitment toward *pro bono* representation. I quenched my parched throat with spring water from the cooler. From their offices on the thirty-ninth floor in the Chrysler Building, everything seemed tragically small and insignificant: the hotdog vendor on the street, the hordes rushing to and from Grand Central Station, the traffic making its way down Lexington Avenue.

The receptionist apprised me that she expected Ms. La Planta any minute. "Can I get you something?" she asked. "Coffee? Soft drink?" I noticed that snacks included easily-masticated biscuits and brownies, no sharp-edge walnuts or pecans to become lodged in the throat.

"Perhaps some tea?" I offered.

I was midway through my cup of green tea when Ms. La Planta returned. "I'll be right with you," she assured me, before disappearing into her office with a stack of message slips.

The receptionist directed me to the conference room, the very room where Ms. La Planta and her colleagues had first appraised my case, informing me that a suit against Seven Happiness was not likely to prevail ("lowballing" client expectations).

A stenography machine had been set up in the room, apparently to simulate the conditions I would face were this an actual deposition.

"Luther." Ms. La Planta whisked into the room. "Sorry to be late. Just putting the terms of a final settlement on the record. Case involving a pedestrian who was struck in the crosswalk at the intersection of Canal and Center Street. Thrown sixty feet in the air before landing on the center median. T-6 fracture of the spinal cord. Meaning he has enough sensation to experience chronic, phantom pain (apparently his leg had been cut off as well), but not enough function to perform the activities of daily living. Where were we? Oh, yes. Deposition preparation. As you can see, we've set up a simulation. You can sit there." She pointed to the head of the table. "The stenographer will be sitting here. She'll administer the oath and will transcribe the proceedings. It's important to VERBALIZE your responses, and to speak clearly and deliberately."

I sat at the head of the table with my hands on my lap.

"No," she corrected me. "Hands folded on the table. Otherwise, you look like you're hiding something. Body language is important, especially if they decide to videotape the deposition, which they've reserved the right to do. In that event, we'll have a further discussion about wardrobe and styling."

I placed my hands on the table as directed.

"During the deposition I will sit by your side, object when appropriate, give you advice on how to respond to questions. However, it's important for you to realize that this deposition is a discovery device purely for the defendant's benefit. It's the defendant's opportunity to probe your knowledge; ideally, to trap you in an admission or account of the facts that you can't disavow later, at least not without being accused of lying. That's their goal, simply put. You have to keep this in mind when answering questions. This is *not* the forum to tell your side of the story. That's the purpose of your testimony at trial, assuming we ever get to trial, which we won't if there's a strategic settlement. Resist the impulse to correct the questioner or to educate him about what happened. It's his job to elicit information, not yours to offer it, unless of course it's information entirely damaging to his case. Then you can offer it gratuitously."

I nodded, though not exactly following.

"Relax," she admonished me. "Your knuckles are turning white. You can't show that level of discomfort, or you'll be prey for Mr. Cushman."

"Mr. Cushman?"

"Stewart Cushman, of Stewart Cushman, P.C., attorneys for Seven Happiness, LLC, and Bernice Wong, the owner of the restaurant. Cushman can be aggressive, intimidating, but he dislikes long depositions. The key is to tire him out before he can elicit any meaningful information."

I released the stress in my fourth metacarpal joint. I was so accustomed to playing the harpsichord, fingering complex parts even when I was away from the instrument, that it was difficult to keep my hands still. "Just the habits of an old musician," I said. "Drumming the fingers, playing harpsichord concerti."

She looked blankly at me. "He's likely to begin with some background questions, your education, your job, where you live, etc. He might try to unnerve you by going for the jugular right away, but generally he likes to stick to a script. He's going to ask a lot of questions about your mother's health and mental status. Resist the impulse to defend your mother or to go overboard with details. Remember, it's not a contest. You're the only one with something to lose. Okay," she said, sipping an herbal tea. "Let's rehearse."

"How old was your mother at the time of death, Mr. van der Loon?"

"Sixty-two years old," I responded.

"Did she suffer from any chronic health problems?" she asked.

"Like what?"

"Diabetes, hypertension, heart arrhythmia?"

"No," I replied.

"How much did she weigh?"

"One hundred forty, one hundred fifty pounds," I guessed. (Obesity, Ms. La Planta was later to educate me, contributes to hypotonicity of the muscles and increases the chance of tongue prolapse, which in turn might exacerbate any tendency to choke upon foreign objects.)

"How much did she drink?" Ms. La Planta asked.

"Not much. A nightly glass of Amaretto. A pitcher of lager if we were celebrating a special occasion at Rolf's Biergarten." (Ms. La Planta raised an eyebrow. "Too much information!" she hissed at me. "And you're not listening to the question – it assumes your mother drank. You fell right into the trap. Try again.")

"How much did she drink?"

"Drink?" I asked innocently. "What do you mean?"

"Alcoholic beverages. How frequently did she drink alcohol?"

"Umm," I paused to reflect, eliminating from my mental calculus the full pitchers of lager we enjoyed on Bavarian night. "Not much, really. An aperitif here and there."

"Did she have a full set of upper and lower teeth?"

"Excuse me?"

"Did she have all of her teeth?"

"Yes, with the exception of a few caps."

"When was the last time she had dental work, prior to the event?"

"I don't recall," I said. I remembered a visit to Dr. Wong-Goldman in early summer, a cleaning during which she was urged to floss more vigorously, lest she succumb to gingivitis. Ms. La Planta held up a hand, signifying that there was no need to elaborate upon my answer.

"Did she take any prescription medications?"

"Um," I said, taking mental inventory of the pills in the medicine cabinet. "Pain relievers, maybe, for arthritic joints. Ginseng as a memory boost."

"So she suffered from arthritis and dementia?"

"No, no," I replied, losing my temper. "Some inflammation of the knuckles, that's all. Her memory was not compromised," I said.

"What about depression?" she asked.

"Depression? Mother was not depressed."

"Her medical records show that she was prescribed SSRIs for what's been described as chronic dysthymia."

"No, no. She was emphatically happy. And she would still be here, if she hadn't choked on your complimentary appetizer."

"Sit down, Luther," Ms. La Planta said, evidently exasperated. "You can't lose your cool like that. It doesn't get us anywhere. Something is bound to come up during the course of the deposition that surprises or infuriates you, but you can't react so negatively. And don't issue spontaneous indictments against Seven Happiness. It just makes you look like you have a vendetta against them. The records do indicate that she was on antidepressants. It's really not relevant. An increase in choking episodes is not seen in this category of pharmaceuticals, so just admit that she was taking them, defuse his argument, and move on." She paused. "Now let's turn to the incident."

"The incident?"

"Obviously he's going to refer to it in neutral terms, 'event,' 'episode,' 'incident,' etc. What do you expect him to say? Fatal choking episode caused by my client's carelessness in food preparation? You can't take that personally. Okay, let's resume." She sighed deeply. "Can you describe for me the events of the night in question?"

"Mother suggested that we order in. She liked the Seven Happiness dinner special. I ordered the glazed duck for me, General Tso chicken for Mother, two small containers of fried rice."

"And this you communicated to the person taking telephone orders?"

"Yes, yes."

"How long did it take for the food to arrive?"

"Let me think," I said, forming a triangle with my thumbs and the tips of my two index fingers. "I would say at least half an hour."

"Half an hour? Or more than half an hour?"

"At least half an hour."

"Can you narrow down the time frame?" Ms. La Planta asked.

"Somewhere between half an hour and an hour."

"Okay, how did you become aware that the food delivery man was on the premises?"

"How? The doorman buzzed to let us know that our take-out had arrived." Jose, in fact – I had forgotten that he was on duty, that he had shown the agent of Mother's destruction to the elevator.

"What happened then?"

"The deliveryman rang the doorbell. He showed me the bill. I gave him forty dollars – he was unable to make change," I said, recalling that I had obscenely tipped him.

"Go on."

"I went to the kitchen to sort out the plates. It was then I noticed the wonton soup. I hadn't realized that it came with the meal, like the fortune cookies. I opened the plastic container of soup and set it before Mother."

"I see. And did you eat some of the wonton soup yourself?" she asked.

"Actually, no," I replied. If I had, perhaps I might have eaten the wayward thatch of bok choy and dumpling.

"Can you describe what the soup looked like?"

"It was just soup. Broth, wontons, bok choy."

"What was inside the wontons?"

"I don't know. Pork, shrimp, something like that."

"But you have no personal knowledge regarding the consistency of the wontons, whether they were tough, or easy to chew?"

"No, but I could see that they were rather–"

"Thank you," she said, cutting me off. "What happened next?"

I popped a grape into my mouth. I tried not to think about what would happen if my gag reflex failed me, if the grape went down the wrong pipe, if I were deprived of oxygen, and no one was there (or at least no one competent enough) to administer the Heimlich maneuver. I put my hands on the seat to steady myself. The clouds drifted by. It all seemed so ludicrously small: Grand Central Station, the buildings on Forty-Second Street, the vista from east to west. "Excuse me," I said. I felt as if someone were sitting on my chest. I tried to breathe but was unable sufficiently to inhale. I felt my pulse, surely one hundred beats per minute or more, resounding in my cranium. The knowledge of ancient systems of neumes, discant style counterpoint, floating in the synapses.

"Have some water," Ms. La Planta offered. I hesitated, unsure of whether the swallowing mechanism would function properly, or I would choke. "Go on," Ms. La Planta encouraged me.

The water dripped down my face as I tried to time swallowing to breaks in respiration. How did the ordinary person do this, many times daily? How did they muster the courage to swallow?

"How often does this happen to you?" Ms. La Planta asked, slipping back into the role of my lawyer, forgoing that of evil interlocutor.

"What?" I choked down the water and wiping the dribble from my chin.

"How often do you experience panic attacks?"

"Not often," I lied. "Just when asked to recount the particulars of Mother's death."

"Well, why don't we take a break and reconvene in a few days' time. We have at least thirty days before we need to produce you. Just take some time to regroup," she said, placing a well-groomed hand on my arm, like she did the first day in the lobby, when she had informally appraised the settlement value of my case. "By the way, have you thought of Xanax?" she asked. "It works wonders. Something to think about, even if it's just to get through the deposition. The receptionist will see you out," she said, turning and clicking her heels. "Take your time."

I decided to go to Rolf's. I proceeded south on Third Avenue. Business owners threw salt on the sidewalk, seeking to avoid, or at least minimize their liability in the event someone slipped and fell. Better to shovel the snow to the side, where it would be someone else's responsibility, or better yet, the City's.

I was alert to the perils of acts as simple as crossing the street, or walking in half-melted snow. Would I ever be able to look upon the world again without thinking through the dangers attendant to every ordinary activity, from walking to crossing the street to eating undercooked, take-out Chinese?

I quickened my step to avoid being hit by a delivery truck. In the months since Mother's death I had become perilously aware of my own mortality – narrowly missing being mowed down by trucks, swerving into embankments on the Vermont-Québec border. It was a means of identifying with what Mother had experienced, of following her to the "other side," of wanting to know Death, which by definition is inscrutable to the living. Though I suffered from ailments of the digestive tract; though I contended with sinuses that did not drain; though my joints and muscles ached from muscular patterns too embedded to undo, my metacarpals destroyed by repetitive attacks upon the keyboard – I had never confronted serious illness, let alone death. I had never contemplated the Beyond, though I frequently played chorales which had as their subject the heavenly host and Our Lord the Redeemer.

Now it seemed as if every hapless stumble from the curb might lead to broken limb. Every street crossing fraught with the possibility of being run over or maimed. Any argument, no matter how trivial – *Did your miniature Doberman leave the present on the sidewalk?* – had the potential for violence and fisticuffs, for which I was ill-equipped to defend myself, since as a harpsichordist I had to protect my hands from insult at all costs. Every time I heard the ambulance screaming down the avenue, *en route* to one of the hospitals along the East Side, I thought of the poor soul inside, strapped to the gurney, pulse failing to register, waiting to be revived with a jolt of epinephrine in the emergency room. I thought of the pedestrian flattened by a hit-and-run driver, limbs disarticulated, lying in the road with a sheet over her body, a warning to the world, *Look away, you want no part of this, those of you who dwell among the living*.

I stopped at the intersection of Third Avenue and Twenty-Sixth Street. It seemed impossible, but Rolf's was gone: the kitschy space, the painted window boxes, the fake chalet façade. The space gutted, the perimeter walled off, pedestrians directed to take the makeshift walkway, else cross to the other side of the street. The murals of the snowy Zugspitze, of the sparkling Danube River and enchanted Bohemian forest – crushed pigments. The long tables and benches on which Mother and I hoisted beer steins – fallen and spent timbers, to be carted off. Nothing to signify what had once been there, just dust, kindling and asbestos-ridden debris.

Gone, gone.

When Mother arrived from Bavaria, in nineteen sixty, she was a girl of just ten. Her widowed father, grieving both a wife and a homeland, had no one to cling to save Mother. *Ich liebe dich*, he told his young daughter, every night before turning in. Within a year, he had remarried a Polish woman, a kind-hearted babka who treated my motherless mother as her own, though her pierogies and borscht, while tasty, evoked nothing for her of the homeland she had lost or the mother who had died, in quarantine at Bellevue Hospital, a victim of tuberculosis and a fatal nostalgia.

One day, walking down Third Avenue, they took a wrong turn and happened upon Rolf's. A biergarten in the middle of New York City, a place evoking a lost world of charming meadows and enchanted forests, of *weisswurst* and dancing around the Maibaum. From then on, Mother and Grandfather frequented Rolf's, spending Sundays eating *weinerschnitzel*, afternoons reading *Abendzeitung*; afternoons, when St. Anastasia let out, Mother did her homework on beer-splattered tables, while grandfather regaled the assembled with renditions of classic *Trinklieder*, timeless songs of heartache and alcohol poisoning.

When Mother wanted to remember Grandfather, she went not to the mausoleum, to replace the desiccated rose and to say a prayer of remembrance; she went to Rolf's on Twenty-Sixth Street. She showed me Grandfather's favorite table. The initials he had carved there over a period of years, painstakingly with a dull butter knife, just to mark his place in the world. When I was a child and Father left us, weighted down with nothing but an old Samsonite case and his own dilapidated spirit, Mother and I consoled ourselves at Rolf's.

I will not here speculate as to the precise nature of the relationship between Mother and Mr. Mueller. Suffice to say, he offered companionship, conversation in the German tongue, and wrote off the bill, else steeply discounted it. He appeared during the holidays with a bottle of Schnapps for Mother and a tin of butter cookies for me. He stayed for an *aperitif,* but always left, Mother's sense of propriety, her loyalty to my absent, presumed dead father precluding any kind of adult sleepover or overture to domesticity.

Mr. Mueller called me "son." *Son, how about some wienerschnitzel? Son, do you need help with the math? How about a game of darts, son?* No one else had ever called me "son." I had no memory of being called son by the father who left us, whom I could no longer recall. (According to Mother, he was responsible not only for leaving us but for my somatic sensitivities: seasonal allergies, sensitivity to light, spasming back, and a sinus condition that kept me awake nights, swallowing the drainage.)

I sank to my knees on the pavement. I could no longer wander into Rolf's, order *Bratkartoffeln,* and sit at the scored table where my Grandfather had carved his initials, lo those many years ago. I could no longer expect to find Mother there, sitting on a bench, enjoying a premium lager, singing *Trinklieder.* I could never again sit at our favorite table, looking for secret messages under the red checked cloth. Life reduced to its simplest terms, I was here, *Ich warum hier.* All of it now rubble, reduced to ash and cartable debris.

"Can I help you?" a young woman inquired, gazing down on me.

"No thank you," I said. "Just having a momentary attack. It will pass."

"Are you sure?" she asked.

"Quite." I stood up and brushed the snow from my kneecaps.

"You don't look well," she said, alluding no doubt to my pallid complexion, the undereye circles (which, following

Mother's death, seemed to be permanently engraved, a marker of my loss).

"I'm okay." I sniffled into the handkerchief I kept stuffed in my pocket to alleviate the infernal sinus drip, the gushes of emotion. Eyes so misty I could not focus, nose so stuffy I could barely breathe, the world wrung of any color or sense. "I'm okay, really." I shooed her away, not wanting her to intrude on my grief, *schmertz*, the vexing fourth stage.

The quarter-comma meantone yielded eight acoustically pure thirds and four howling "wolfes." In practical terms, this meant that certain thirds – B-D#, D-flat-F, F#-A# – were never sounded; certain keys, those with sharps or more than two flats, never used.

Sounds out of reach, hovering in the aural spectrum.

22.

I played the sarabande from one of Bach's dance suites, then the cadenza from the fifth Brandenburg concerto, impervious to Mrs. Hildebrandt pounding on the wall. It was not yet ten o'clock, the hour at which the rules of the cooperative forbade the playing of "loud stereos" or "musical instruments." The harpsichord in any event is a dynamically limited instrument, unlike its cousin the piano-forte; it is meant to be played in an intimate setting, not a concert hall; it is meant to complement a virginal or lute, not an orchestra. The harpsichord is notoriously sensitive, not the least because its strings are wound near the breaking point. Mrs. Hildebrandt had no reason to complain, and in addition was our last remaining rent-controlled tenant, so her complaints to the management company went entirely unheeded.

"I'm going to play you a gigue, Mrs. Hildebrandt," I said, a buoyant piece in 6/8 time. Mrs. Hildebrandt was at least ninety years old. She had no children, just a niece who visited on occasion, and a social worker who saw to it that she received the full complement of elder care services. She had a fetid, yapping terrier, which she allowed to void in a clay litter box, as if a domesticated cat. Why had this wretch survived long past any reasonable expiration date, when Mother – full of life, eagerly anticipating a lecture on Wagner's Venetian exile at the

Morgan Library – had been cut down prematurely? Though I knew, logically, that Mrs. Hildebrandt had nothing to do with Mother's demise, that did not prevent me from blaming her or using her as a focal point for my rage.

At ten o'clock, I shut the lid and placed the dust cover on Aveline. I stayed up reading, perusing Mother's *Pictorial History of Bavaria*, a weighty tome she had possessed since childhood. I had looked through it many times, imagining Mother as a girl, inhaling fresh Alpine air. I could detect a molecule of her in the atmosphere, a whiff of perfume, the light gardenia scent she preferred.

I decided to have a light snack before turning in, warm milk and chocolate chip cookies. I removed a china plate from the shelf, Mother's preferred pattern, blue Asiatic Pheasant. As I was about to exit the kitchen, I espied, crumpled in the trash, Chinese iconography I knew all too well. A plastic bag from Seven Happiness Chinese takeout, containing the remnants of fried rice and dumplings.

"Cecilia!" I shouted accusatorily, "What have you done?" I dragged the bag behind me, heedless of the soy sauce dripping on the floor, the fortune cookies crumbling underfoot as I stomped into the bedroom. "What's this?" I demanded, lifting up the offending bag.

She blushed but quickly recovered. "What? I'm not allowed to go there? They should be shunned forever? It's bad enough they won't deliver here anymore and that I had to pick it up at the restaurant. It's not their fault, Luther. It's not your mother's, and it's not yours. It was just an accident." She had a morsel of pork stuck between her teeth, which would have given her away, even if I hadn't happened upon the bag.

"Yes, they should be shunned. Why would it be Mother's fault, for God's sake? Why would you say that? She was the victim!"

"But you blame her Luther, don't you? You blame her for leaving you alone. You're forty years old, but essentially you're an infant. You've never lived apart from her (Not true: I spent a year abroad, studying the Wolfenbüttel Codex.) You refuse to displace her, to remove even one thing of hers from this apartment. It's one of the most extreme cases of mummification I've ever seen."

"Don't analyze my stages of grief!" I snapped at her.

"It's been seven months. She's not coming back, Luther. She's never coming back. She's passed to the other side. She's made a transition from this life to the next, depending on what your belief system is –"

"You think the Hereafter is the product of our selective belief systems? That there is no Hereafter for the atheist because he doesn't believe in it, but one for the faithful Christian, who lives this life in apprehension of the glorious one to follow?"

"You're intellectualizing now. You're distancing yourself from your own loss, though you're entombed with her, too. You have to acknowledge the loss before you can grieve it," she said, no doubt parroting from Chapter 1 of the manual. "It's not disrespectful to order from Seven Happiness, Luther. I'm just sick of Thai Kitchen."

She had consumed the entire meal, leaving only one, neatly pinched dumpling. It was a vivid reminder of all I had lost and the stupidity of Mother's passing – if only I had apprehended the danger in the bitter green vegetable, which Mother would always chew for "digestive and bowel health" – and I resented Cecilia for it.

"You're angry that I chose to live with Mother, rather than you. That you lived and worked in that office filled with ethnic totems and books about death and dying. That we never married, despite your disparagement of the institution as an anthropological convention designed to foster procreation and to stave off the inevitability of death. Of course, if I had just thrown Mother in the crematorium, rather than interring her 'shell' in an Eternal Bronze casket, we might have had enough money to go to the Caribbean during the winter, rather than renting a room in Micheline's Québécois funhouse."

The Victorian sofa – to which I was banished – provided little buffer for my spasm-wracked lower back. In the morning, Cecilia was gone. The one drawer in the bureau I had allotted her – admittedly not enough space for her flowing scarves and globular costume jewelry – emptied out. Gone was the *Directory of Thanatologists* and the two-faced Kali puppet, one face the serene mediator, the other the hideous destroyer.

23.

The gravesite is meant to provide solace to those left behind. Those who need a body and a coffin, those for whom cremation is anathema, a relic of the old Catholic belief that bodies needed to be "preserved" (hah) for the Day of Judgment – when, like our Lord Savior Jesus Christ, they would be resurrected from their graves, throw off their death shrouds (in the case of the modern corpse, a suit or best dress, of the "mother of the bride" variety), and ascend to Heaven in a blaze of glory. The Catholic Church has since decreed that cremation is an acceptable practice, despite pulverization of remains that makes it impossible, in theory, for the corpse to rise from the dead.

I knelt on the velvet padded kneeler, head between my hands, wondering what I was supposed to do. Scream for the mother who had prematurely choked to death, in an accident wholly avoidable had I ordered instead from Marimba Sushi? Curse the universe that had taken from me my only family member, the one person who had loved me unquestioningly (accepting my dedication to Renaissance music, rather than to the Romantic era of which she was fond), who filled the void left by Father's precipitous departure as best she could, never blaming me for her predicament?

I came seeking solace (and to replenish the flowers in the crypt, already looking haggard after the passage of a week), but there was none to be found. Her name had yet to be chiseled in by the stonemason. For now, her grave remained unmarked, uninscribed, known only to the keepers of the cemetery plot and to me, the one she had left behind when she decided to choke on a wonton.

I rose, said my superfluous farewells, and locked the door to the crypt behind me. The groundskeepers were backfilling a new grave, replenishing the soil and smoothing it over. Rest in peace, or at least until another one of your family members dies, and his coffin is stacked atop yours, cemetery overcrowding an unfortunate fact of life for anyone expiring within the city limits.

The groundskeeper idled his engine, evidently not wanting to disturb me by exposing me to the rougher elements of the trade, the vaults thrown open, the crude backfill.

Despite seeing the public service announcement for *How to render aid to a choking victim* behind the counter, something I unwittingly gazed upon while waiting for extra duck sauce, instructions I half-memorized while demanding extra packets of soy – double-fist, position here – I fumbled. Others are able to achieve focus in moments of crisis, to undergo metamorphoses from clumsy underachievers to heroes possessed of superhuman strength. Not I. Following many years in which I suffered from stage fright, shaking merely to perform the Roman de Fauvel before an audience of ten to fifteen bored academicians, I simply froze.

Resume your backfilling operations, I say. Drink the coffee from your thermos, guffaw with your buddies, and return tomorrow to dig a fresh grave.

"Don't fall in," the groundskeeper warned, as I stumbled over the ruptured ground.

24.

As an assistant professor of an obscure branch of musicology, I was not deemed an essential member of the department capable of deciding its fate nor the particulars of its curricula. I was not allowed to judge auditions, or to grade pupils on their performances, my vitriolic feelings towards the equal temperament thought to influence my judgment in matters of technique and repertoire. My exile to the Fenster Wing summed up the generally held view of me as a Renaissance recluse, a nuisance with period instruments. Save for the obligatory faculty recital, during which I played the coda from the Fifth Brandenburg concerto (not in equal temperament), I was left to my minimal teaching responsibilities and organization of the annual Early Music Symposium.

I was mildly alarmed when Burt expressed an urgent need to see me. I would have missed the message entirely had I not been sitting in my office during desolate regularly scheduled office hours, waiting for a student to rap upon the door, seeking clarification on the rules of counterpoint.

Burt was a trombonist. He liked to remind me that his musical education began with Bach and the equal temperament (adhering to the fiction, propagated by misinformed musicologists, that Bach was the father of the equal temperament, when nothing could be further from the truth: Bach wrote in an irregular, shifting temperament known as well-temperament, *wohltempiert*, similar to extended sixth comma meantone but assuredly *not* the equal temperament) and was of the belief that failing to learn earlier musical styles had not in any way compromised his musical development nor rendered his ear insensitive.

"Come in," Burt motioned.

I hesitated. The walls were lined with various plaques of commendation, liner notes from several of his albums (he was a session musician on tracks for more notable performers), battered copies of the "Fake Book," or the "Real Book," the spiral bound bible of improvising musicians. I entered with trepidation and assumed the chair across from his desk. The Fake Book was open to *My Funny Valentine*.

"Luther, you know my job as head of the department has its unpleasant side." He ruminated. "Students who play in rock bands and don't know a thing about harmonic progression. Students who can't read simple melodies, let alone improvise over chord changes. The arts aren't a high priority here. We're not Julliard, after all. Kids come here to study music, but with a safety net, to get a B.A. in some social science so they can go on to law school or a social work profession. What I'm trying to say is, they've cut funding for the department yet again. They're giving all the money to the business school. I've had to make some tough choices. So after this year, no more symposium. It's become cost-prohibitive to house these players and transport their instruments from Bavaria or Austria-Hungary or wherever they come from, and to arrange for proper instrument storage. Especially since attendance at the event is nil, even with the promise of school credit." Like most players who spent hours on their embouchure, Burt had a bad habit of pursing his lips.

"Since we're eliminating the symposium, you'll be assigned other responsibilities," including, apparently, the teaching of non-credit courses to nonmatriculated students in the Division of Continuing Education. Music Appreciation (avoiding discussion about the nature of harmony and refraining from injecting any "personal" opinions concerning the nature of tonality), and (since the Division of Continuing Ed was largely populated by retired seniors) Beginner Piano for the arthritic and hard of hearing.

I nodded. I might have railed against the lack of university support, accused Burt of being a craven Romanticist. I might have accused him of being a sell-out, more interested in hobnobbing with the university trustees, and nibbling on reheated quiche.

But instead I said nothing. *The grief-stricken patient experiences many phases while learning to integrate the loss of the loved one, including debilitating malaise and an obdurate form of resignation. The grieving patient extrapolates his own, private pain onto the world around him, believing he is acutely vulnerable to loss. Whereas once he might have felt competent, or at least not lackluster, he instead feels inept, powerless to fend of the accumulating losses, experiencing what might be viewed as an unraveling. Everything falls apart.* I stared out the window at Washington Square Park. The Arch, modeled after the Arc de Triomphe, presiding over a barren world.

I left, a sheaf of counterpoint exercises under my arm. I did not want to go home, to be reminded by the lingering scent of incense and the left-behind library of grief (*Stages of Grief, Working through Grief, The Grieving Analysand, East Coast Directory of Thanatologists*) of Cecilia's absence. I did not want to order take-out, to be reminded of the fatal moment when a wonton lodged itself in Mother's throat, rendering her mute, unable to communicate her distress (save for a desperate pantomime, hands clutching her neck), while I stood by, powerless to do anything, my attempts at the Heimlich maneuver, like my desire to compose in the Renaissance style using obsolescent systems of tuning, an exercise in futility.

I decided to go to the Irish pub down the street. I hoisted a pint or two in Mother's memory (no one was listening; a college basketball game droned in the background). Soon, I found myself flanked by an outer-borough woman of a certain age. Wonderment at the care lavished on her nail appliqués (which became awe when I learned that she was a professional typist), soon turned to lurid, drunken discussion. I wasn't accustomed to meeting members of the opposite sex, let alone consorting in bars, in an atmosphere conducive to casual fornication. My new friend ("Cheri") dug her nails into my arm, hand fed me a chicken wing dripping with lurid orange sauce, and suggested that we have some "fun." Nothing of the sort had happened to me since I'd picked up a Burgundian lady of the night during my doctoral studies. I had no reason to refuse. Cecilia had abandoned me, and I no longer had a mother whose sensibilities I was afraid of offending.

Jose (who was working a double shift) looked the other way when I arrived home with my companion. The elevator arrived quickly and spirited us upstairs. I offered to regale Cheri with a period harpsichord piece. She declined and proceeded to remove my clothing. Cecilia preferred to recline on the bed, semi-naked, while I sloughed off sweater vest and trousers.

Cheri threw me on the bed and swallowed me whole.

I felt as if I ought to offer her a refreshment, but did not want to interrupt her momentum. I feared that if I startled her she might sever a tender vesicle with her studded fingernail.

It was taking awhile, this I sensed. She was remarkably cheerful, considering the kneeling position she was required to maintain on the brusque Flemish wool rug.

"Do you have a beer?" she asked abruptly, coming up for air.

"I think there might be an ale in the refrigerator," I replied, sprawled in naked ignominy on my child's bed, too embarrassed to get up and be thrown into the spotlight of the refrigerator.

I awaited her return, ludicrously erect yet unable to climax. Cheri took a swig of beer and set to work again, using mouth and hands in exhilarating, coordinated tandem, a feat I could only admire as an advocate of vigorous keyboard technique. I closed my eyes and allowed my bitter cum to flow into her mouth, to be drained from me and to cause me no more angst.

I'd hoped that a proffer of cab fare would send her on her way, back to the outerborough from whence she came, but she wanted to stay the night. She assumed, as would any sane adult, that Mother's bedroom – the one with the full-size bed, coverlet and pillow shams – was mine, and mine that of a child who visited every other weekend. Before I could explain that the full-size bed had belonged to my mother, that the apparatus of my grief precluded me from sleeping in her bed, that I suffered from anxiety attacks that left me breathless and awake, unable to sleep without pharmacological assistance – Cheri passed out. I left her on the twin bed, unbuttoning her skin-tight jeans to enable her better to respire.

I considered what to do. I had long resisted sleeping in Mother's bed – maintaining it in the same condition as the last night she had slept in it, down to the fusty sheets and the ear wax on the pillow sham. I had left the bed unmolested for eight months – enough time, assuredly, to assuage the guilt I felt in connection with her ludicrous demise.

With trepidation, I slipped in. I pulled the coverlet up to my neck. Yet sleep eluded me.

I tried to distract myself by working out new fingerings for the Brandenburg cadenza in my head, mental exercise I had hoped would divert and exhaust me. However, I found myself still awake.

I wandered into the kitchen to fix myself a snack. When I was a boy, and accursed post-nasal drip, together with apnic breathing (a deviated septum, an obstructive uvula), kept me awake nights, Mother would make me a snack – chocolate chip cookies and a warm glass of milk – to soothe me and help me fall back asleep. Little of the ritual had changed over the years. Warm milk became a snifter of bourbon, and my insomniac musings (Had I properly classified the specimen as belonging to the morpho genus?), now veered toward matters of life and death, speculations with no straightforward answers, no compendium of North American butterflies containing the relevant information in easy-to-follow chart form. Opening the freezer, I encountered the *bûche de Noël* (Micheline's frosty note still attached), a piece of layer cake from Cecilia's and my last, fraught anniversary (neither of us had an appetite after arguing about whether an individual had a right to bury his loved ones as he chose, a freedom usurped by mortuary associations), but could not, despite ransacking the contents of the freezer, find the container of wonton soup.

Had I disposed of it while sleepwalking? Had I eaten it myself (as a member of a primitive society might), as if by doing so I could achieve symbolic mastery over death, commune with Mother by reenacting her final act on this earth?

I sank to the floor, head between my hands. In moments of crisis we are overwhelmed by the impulse to sink to the ground. Cowering from the truth, avoiding the inevitable – *Yes,*

*I'll sign to allow transport of the body; please, please, do not pro-
nounce her dead on the spot.*

Whence I espied a plastic container in the trash. A leaf of
bok choy pressed against the interior. The crystallized broth of
Mother's last, fatal meal.

Oh, what had you done, vile vixen! I tried to salvage what
had been left of the soup, but it was useless. Nothing remained.
It had been thoroughly masticated and swallowed, Cheri in her
drunken state somehow able to digest the doughy wontons —
frozen no less — that had been Mother's undoing.

I strode into the bedroom and shook her awake. "Did you
eat the wonton soup?" I demanded, holding the hollowed-out
container.

"I guess. I don't know. I don't really remember," she half-
smiled, eyes crusted with left-over makeup.

"Please leave," I implored, the world spinning around me.
I felt I would lose my balance and crumble to the ground.

"Hey, why don't we get some breakfast or something?" she
mumbled, slowly awakening. "We had some fun last night,
huh?" One of her nails had flaked off in the bed, a palm on a
beach with a golden-studded sun.

"I need you to leave," I said, still clutching the container,
the defrosted remnants of my mother's last meal exposed to
room temperature and rapidly decaying — as assuredly as was
her corpse, despite Mr. M.'s representations regarding the effi-
cacy of the embalming process.

"You're weird," she accused me, as she rose and struggled
with the zipper on her too-tight jeans. "Even if I ate your Chinese food, so what? You can just order in more," she said, un-
knowingly, not realizing that the emptied-out container was
irreplaceable, the last item with which Mother had had earthly
contact.

"Go," I whimpered.

"Can I just pee, for Christ's sake?" she asked. She half-closed the door and released a stream of liquid containing the metabolized contents of Mother's final repast.

Ms. La Planta was furious about "spoliation" of the wonton soup. It had been her intent to show, by dramatic comparison to another, nonfatal serving, that the wontons in the soup Mother had ingested were doughy and difficult to masticate, that the profusion of bok choy, in seaweed like clumps, only increased the danger presented by the soup, vegetation which in isolation or (in Mother's case) by entanglement with other elements in the soup heightened the danger that an unsuspecting individual would choke while eating.

I hesitated to tell my attorney than an uncultivated woman had eaten the soup in an inebriated state and had not suffered any harm. I felt anger toward Mother. Why couldn't she adequately masticate the wontons, when Cheri, despite the extent of her drunkenness, had eluded its destructive potential?

"Your deposition has been scheduled for next month," Ms. La Planta informed me. "We're going to have to rehearse again. When you're ready. Have you taken my suggestion and gotten Xanax?"

"I'm fine," I lied.

25.

Given the budgetary constraints on this, the last Early Music Symposium, I could not afford passenger tickets for the instruments. I was forced to consign them to cargo, and hope they'd arrive intact, none the worse for wear for enduring the temperature and pressure fluctuations in the hold. The manifest indicated that I was to expect several split keyboard variants, an upright clavichord, a clavicytherium, a virginal, and a refurbished seventeenth century harpsichord, of the Flanders variety.

The airport's cargo areas were vast and sprawling, located along a ring road. I felt, with each revolution, that I was descending further into a transportational hell, an endlessly repeating figure with little variation, much like a fifteenth-century fugue. At last I espied the offices of the carrier, set back from the road. The instruments had indeed arrived the night previous, but would not be released to me until I obtained the stamp of the custom's official and paid any applicable duty.

"Fine," I sighed. "Please direct me to customs."

Upon arriving at the designated floor of the customs building I had to wait in line an additional thirty minutes before a uniformed official, increasingly frustrated that he could not find "period instruments" among his objects on which to levy duty – decided to charge me $6. I was instructed to present my receipt to the clerk in shipping to prove that I had paid the fee and had not cheated the United States government of a significant income stream associated with unregulated traffic in period instruments.

When finally I arrived at shipping, the clerk accepted my stamped declaration and directed me to the warehouse, where my shipment had been organized on the loading dock. "This yours?" a worker asked.

"I believe so," I said. This prolonged contact with the hubs of transportation had left me exhausted.

It was the first time I had ventured into Queens for a purpose other than going to the cemetery. A borough shadowed by the flight paths of domestic and international air traffic, and peppered with ethnic eating establishments that unfortunately recalled for me the unhappy circumstances of Mother's death. It seemed wrong to be in Queens and not to see Mother. In my mind, the association would always be there: the hearse, the funeral procession, the coffin with the air lock I later discovered to be a gimmick sold to grieving wretches like myself.

"Forgive me, Mother." I whizzed by on the highway, trying to discern the family mausoleum amidst the sea of gravestones and monuments, the stone angels and chiseled columns that reached heavenward while their foundations insidiously rotted, erosion hastened by the cemetery's proximity to tanks spewing their toxic fumes.

Dear Ernst,

You have accused me of being a latter day Zarlino, of being consumed by "magic numbers." If I am Zarlino, you are the ruthless Galilei, treacherous student who published the scurrilous Dialogo of 1581, attacking his mentor's ideas regarding the Pythagorean proportions and advocating for musical anarchy. What is to be gained from such musical relativism, I ask you? (It is just as well you are not coming to this year's Early Music Symposium. Your intolerance for any temperament other than the equal temperament would tax the spirit of scholarship and free exchange of ideas the symposium is intended to foster.)

26.

By this point in the year, we were to have covered the Roman mass, the Micrologus of Guido d'Arezzo, the French Ars Nova, and Guillaume de Machaut, the greatest of the Renaissance composer-performers. But I had barely made it through Chapter 3, *Displacement Syncopation*, exhausted by questions of tonality and temperament.

"Let's go to the Hairy Monk," I offered. The class would soon be over. The final exam – compose a motet in the style of Machaut – administered and generously graded. The course evaluations – all three – deposited anonymously in a box in the office. Perhaps I might catch a set by William's band at a dive bar located off Avenue D. More likely, I would see him at the Tiki Burger, grilling to regulation medium (so as to destroy *e. coli* bacteria), staking paper umbrellas in the buns, as per franchise regulations that dictated everything from the appearance of the burger to the number of napkins that had to be stuffed in the dispenser.

"I propose a toast," I said. "A medieval blessing, as best I remember it

Each must drain his cup of wine,
And I the first will toss off mine:

Thus I advise,
Here then I bid you all Wassail,
Cursed be he who will not say Drink Hail.

"Here, here," they said, raising their glasses. They thanked me for the spirited discussions and for grading their counterpoint exercises on a generous curve, for exposing them to the grand debates of Zarlino and Galilei and for taking heat from the animal rights protestors (it was my digitized photograph, alas, that had been snapped during the protest and uploaded to the Animal Liberation Organization website; I who had been described as an "Animal Butcher," a high-ranking enemy of the cause, just behind Dr. Xiao Wu, chimpanzee lobotomist). Twenty years from now, who knew where they'd be. Frankie might find herself in a hospice, playing acoustic guitar for the terminally ill. Nazif might succeed in cornering the ethnic techno market. William might become a speed metal sensation, playing grunge fests from Hamburg to Manila, or he might cut his hair and accept full-time employment at Kinko's.

In the end, we would all die, be waked in business attire (gentleman's suit and tie, tea-length dress for the ladies) or cremated straightaway, our loved ones presented with a bronze cup of cremains, a handsome urn that could be displayed on the fireplace, handed down from generation-to-generation, else its contents scattered across the waters in a sensitive ceremony filled with off-key hymnals and the infernal, twentieth-century trope, *Wind Beneath My Wings*. What did it matter, when all would be forgotten? These days at the university, the pitchers of lager at the Hairy Monk, the ghoulish Fenster Wing, with its flickering white lights and soundproofed torture chambers. It would all fade away eventually, flash and disappear, white light indicative of nothing more than brain death, oxygen-starved neurons. Our memories ablated as assuredly as those of the laboratory rats in Room 242, who could no longer find their way through the maze, who hurled themselves against the sides of the wall, unable, ever, to return "home" (the sadistic starting point where a hunk of cheese awaited them).

We would be lucky if we merited a footnote, somewhere, citation in an academic journal, an annotation in a textbook, some acknowledged contribution. *Pre-mensural Notation* was still incomplete, abandoned after a succession of disappointing events: my *ennui* in Toulouse; the destruction of the Montpellier Codex after a malfunction with the sprinkler system. Alas, my finest contribution to the scholarship remains *Motet Structure in the Roman de Fauvel*, a second-rate survey of a seminal work of the French Ars Nova.

Who had ever heard of Francesco Landini? The songs of Jehan de Lescurel? Who, other than a handful of pathetic musicologists, could sing a madrigal? Tune a virginal? Who could speak to the rhythmic complexities reflected in the normal mensurations? Who, other than a sad professor of medieval and Renaissance music, would know that the sacred tones had been tampered with, that the sonorities we accepted as true, as real, were nothing more than tonal perversions devised by a medieval lunatic intent on hacking up the Pythagorean comma?

The simple, most literal, analysis of *Free Bird* is that of breakup, literal leave-taking. The anthem is, on another level, a tribute to a dead band member, a metaphysical reflection on what awaits us after death. Though expressed in rather cliché terms, obvious metaphors (*free bird*, etc.), the song lyrics nonetheless touch on deep emotions, speak to a human need to honor those who have gone before, whether felled prematurely by small plane crash (We're having trouble landing! Can't clear the tree line!, I have taken liberties in reconstructing the tragedy) or by foreign body airway obstruction (My mother is dying! Please hurry!, She's choking on a wonton!, the verbatim transcription of my 911 call, placed at 6:44 EST, according to dispatch records).

"I'm gonna miss this class," William said.

"It is true, the dying prefer Just intervals," said Frankie, who was working with hospice patients.

If I leave here tomorrow,
would you still remember me?

"I will miss all of you," I said, a tear appearing in my eye. The sky darkened and the air grew thick, as it did before humid downpour. I told the barkeep that the next round was on me.

27.

I found myself wandering the campus, stricken with nostalgia. This was the same campus, after all, where I had pursued my undergraduate studies, assiduously practicing the harpsichord while others pounded on the ostentatiously dynamic *piano-forte*, drowning poor technique in heavy sustain pedaling. The harpsichord is dynamically-limited; the manner in which the keys are activated (by plectra rather than percussive hammers) does not allow for dynamic range. Still, I was beguiled by its sound-making properties, the rigors of its tone. I learned, during my apprenticeship, how the harpsichord was crafted, the mysterious elements of its sound, more practical skills such as how to tune the instrument (it was far easier to tune than its modern descendant, the *piano-forte*, requiring only calibration at the bridge and attention to the plectra, which need frequent replacement).

I had little time for socialization, shunning mixers and other events involving alcoholic depredations, finding solace instead in the chipped keys of the harpsichord, the Italian-style instrument I had before Aveline.

I was abstemious throughout college. My only interlude of note a brief liaison with a waif I had encountered in Washington Square Park. I suspected Veronica of being underage, despite the professional quality identification card she carried on her person. These forgeries were a dime a dozen on Eighth Street, where new identities were minted in the back rooms of tattoo parlors and lingerie shops. We cavorted in the park, frolicked naked in the mews, the liberality of our explorations enhanced by what were, at the time, lax security practices and an aura of free-spirited investigation. One day she failed to appear at our designated meeting spot under the Arch, and I was made to draw my own devastating inferences. Having a father who did not give us the courtesy of a bloated body or even a whitewashed bone – leaving us instead to bureaucratic presumptions – had stirred in me anxieties about absence and the prospect of return.

It was easier to date surreptitiously than to bear the crushing weight of Mother's disapproval. No one was ever good enough; none my intellectual equal; no one understood my musical temperament; no one understood my excruciating sensitivities, the rhinitis, the allergies, the sinus plaints that contributed to my sour mood and necessitated nasal sprays and Neti pots. My "love life" was carried on secretly, in musty library stacks, on dormitory futons, in cramped practice rooms that had the virtue of soundproofing.

In my twenties, I studied in ducal libraries, dissected medieval organs to discover the secrets of their tuning, and lived with cloistered monks to save on expenses. It was one of the happiest times of my life: awoken by the *matinales*, lulled to sleep by vespers, discerning in the contrapuntal lines of the church offices something of the divine. I studied Wolfenbüttel I in a temperature-controlled room, using tongs so as not to befoul its pages with my unclean digits. Ah, to be so close to Leonin and Perotin, the fathers of polyphony! I was seized by an abiding love for this early music, so rigidly formulaic and yet so free, voices soaring above a basso continuo, neumes springing to life from illuminated manuscripts. I might have stayed forever, in a Burgundian farmhouse or in a less austere cell of the monastery. But I was tethered to Mother, for whom unexpected disappearances had already taken a toll. And so I returned, completing my doctoral dissertation on *Premensural Notation in Early Sources of Notre Dame Polyphony*.

Mother, of course, never dated. I suspected, for a while, that she was carrying on a furtive romance with Reginald, a neighbor of ours and a fellow member of the Tudor Greens Society. He feigned an interest in the *hydrangea anomala*, I am certain, merely to get close to her. But her heart was thorny and closed, presumptions of death notwithstanding.

She was fond of Mr. Mueller, the proprietor of Rolf's, for he evoked the memory of the homeland she had left behind. He conversed with her in the Bavarian dialect and made *Leberkäse*. But she never took his overtures seriously, ascribing his attentions, his presents of Bavarian trinkets, to overzealous friendship. Having experienced the disappearance of one man – never a note, never a missive from the beyond, to let her know that he was still alive, somewhere in time – she was reluctant to entrust her affections to another. She remained guarded until the end of her days, suspicious of men's motives, unwilling to embark on more than a trivial affair (and on these, her fastidious diary is silent).

The campus has not changed much. The Arch, modeled after its French counterpart, looms above the park. I sat under the shade of an ashleaf maple, the same tree under which I contemplated, during long afternoons in Washington Square, the nature of the diesis, the mysteries of tonality, where, in Greenwich Village, one might purchase a mesolabium (answer: antique shop on the corner of Third Street and Sixth

Avenue). It seems to me that time is not a finite progression, ever onwards, but a series of recursive passages, events we keep stumbling over, recurring motifs, chords that never satisfactorily resolve.

28.

I scheduled another appointment for deposition preparation, after having procured anti-anxiety medication from my physician.

Ms. La Planta tottered into the room on stilettos, dipping bag of green tea. "I have to cut back on caffeine," she explained. "All right, Luther, let's pick up where we left off. You were describing the events leading up to the fatal incident. Your Mother ordered General Tso chicken. The meal came with a complimentary bowl of wonton soup. Where were you sitting?" she asked.

"Mother was sitting at her usual place at the head of the dining table. I sat next to her, at a right angle."

"Okay. Please describe what happened next."

"Mother had just started eating the soup. She asked me what was in it. I shrugged. Pork, I imagined. She had a few sips of the broth. I noticed her cautiously nibbling on a wonton."

I paused. The moment seemed to advance frame by frame, in agonizing stillness, every grimace, sharp inhalation, gradation of coloring, from healthy pink to white to blue-tinged. Would she live, cough up the fatal plug? Or would it insinuate itself deeper, choke her of air? The dividing line between this world and what lies beyond – if indeed there is a realm beyond our apprehension – so permeable that a misdirected wonton, in less than thirty seconds, could end this Life.

"She started chewing. She seemed to enjoy it. Then she gulped. I was startled, because Mother was not a noisy eater." I remembered a high-pitched whine, the E above middle C, as the wonton caught her unawares.

"She pointed to her throat. She couldn't speak. I asked whether she was choking and she nodded. She started turning blue. I went behind her and drove my fist into her stomach, tried to perform the Heimlich maneuver, but nothing."

I punched so hard into her belly, trying to expel the wonton, that I lifted her off the floor. One-TWO, one-TWO. I imagined Marlene's students enacting the rhythmic sequence in Dalcroze eurhythmics, drawing themselves up, collapsing on the floor. By the third or fourth thrust she was limp, slack-jawed, lifeless.

Somehow, in the midst of this, I managed to call 911, to calmly inform them of my emergency, *My mother is choking, please hurry.* How was it possible that all of this was simultaneously occurring? Two voices, moving together and apart according to the rules of counterpoint. The operator warned against performing a blind sweep of the airway, cautioning me that doing so would only drive the object deeper. I said I understood, then proceeded to pry Mother's jaws open, to peer inside the convulsing throat, to thrust my fingers in, hoping to find the foreign body, or at least stimulate a gag reflex that would cause her to regurgitate the item. This information I withheld from Ms. La Planta as not pertinent, ashamed that I might have hastened Mother's demise by my inappropriate actions contrary to all protocols for the choking victim, which dictate that one never attempt to fish a foreign object out of the airway unless it is clearly visible and able to be extracted.

"The paramedics arrived. One of them initiated CPR. But he could not revive her." Mother was already nonresponsive, pupils fixed and dilated, vacant. She remained propped in a chair, slumped over. Plundered take-out on the table; plum sauce dripping on the floor; fortune cookies crushed underfoot.

I put my hand on the table to steady myself. I had lost the ability to judge distance or to perceive depth, the proportions of the room warped and dissembling. The rules of counterpoint had developed over centuries, built on the solidity of the perfect intervals. The octave, the fifth, and the fourth: proportions divined by Ptolemy in the elliptical motions of heavenly bodies. Yet even these fixed oscillations were revealed to be relative, dependent on variables such as string length and material, and other, unaccountable acoustical phenomena.

I sipped water from a glass, trying to swallow without thinking about it. Thirty-six muscles are implicated in the act of swallowing. Miraculous, really, that more people did not choke, given the concerted muscular effort needed merely to swallow.

I was conscious of my breathing. I felt my heart would stop.

"Are you okay?" Ms. La Planta asked, refilling my water glass.

"I think so."

"You did it," she congratulated me. "That was the most difficult part. The rest will be easy." She squeezed the last drops of flavor from her tea.

29.

Spring: the promise of new life, before everything becomes bone-crushing dispiritedness. I wandered into the south park and sat on a bench. Two trees had been planted in Mother's honor. She would be pleased that her name was linked, in eternity, with the garden she so loved, a perennial reminder of her span on this Earth.

I walked along the gravel path, looking for the brass plaque the Tudor Greens Society had dedicated to her memory. I remember little of how I stumbled through the first days and weeks, attempting to replicate the actions of a normal human being, one whose mother had not been wrenched from him in a choking accident described by the emergency medical crew as FBAO, dead on arrival.

I became accustomed to seeing her life bracketed in time, hearing her referred to as "deceased," or "late," words signifying her mortal terminus. I thought of the overtone series: perfect ratios, sympathetic wave forms, the whole of the aural spectrum. I thought of Mother as a shimmering octave, vibrating somewhere in the universe, beyond my apprehension.

I found the brass plaque beneath some undergrowth. I cleared away the vines, seeing her name, Celeste van der Loon, Faithful Friend of the Tudor Greens Society. It was etched in brass, a sturdy metal. It might one day oxidize but it would remain a long while. It comforted me to know that there were some things that had at least the veneer of permanence, of being immutable.

Returning home, I encountered one of Cecilia's patients in the lobby. He was sitting dejectedly on the pew, rubbing his eyes, awaiting appraisal of his Stages of Grief and prospects for healing. *Go now*, I wanted to say. *It's no use. The dead are no longer with us, but their presence is oppressive, an undertow, pulling us into the next world, if indeed there is one.*

30.

Piccolo Fabrizzi was scheduled to arrive via Alitalia, a bulk-head seat so that in case of emergency he would be the first to exit the plane, and would not have to worry about losing his orientation in a smoke-filled cabin full of stampeding passengers. Piccolo had been involved in several emergency landings, heightening his paranoia about air travel and prospects for arriving intact.

I e-mailed Piccolo a schematic of the airline cabin, highlighting both the ease of escape and the seats with extra legroom. I recommended that he perform stretching exercises on an hourly basis so as to prevent clot formation. "Raise and lower the leg at regular intervals," I advised. "Rotate the ankle joint," I recommended, sending him a link to a site for Deep Vein Thrombosis ("DVT"), hoping to educate without contributing to hypochondria.

Now that Mother was gone, and Cecilia too, with her morbid tomes and prescriptions about the grieving process, there was nothing to prevent me from inviting Piccolo to stay at the apartment. Nothing, save my inability to sleep in my dead Mother's bed and my failure to acclimate to life without her. (I went so far as to dedicate my nightly renditions of trouvère songs to Mother, exclaiming, while playing, *Did you enjoy that?*, *The transition could be smoother, no?*, *I'm still having difficulty with the meter*, as if she were still there, sipping tea from a cracked Asiatic Pheasant cup, counting the measures, applauding enthusiastically when I reached the end. *Bravo*.)

"You're welcome to stay here, Piccolo. I have an extra room for guests. It should be quite comfortable." So long as I managed to surmount my anxieties and learned to sleep in Mother's bed. I could not suggest that he and I, like monks at L'Abbeye de Clairval, sleep nestled in my twin bed, struggling for mattress space.

"That is kind of you my friend. It will save me much grief acclimating to the hotel," he replied. "I accept."

My usual practice session, two to three hours of Baroque dance forms and harpsichord cadenzas, ran to four; my fingers, though callused from years of play, were near bleeding; my eyes, middle aged and presbyopic, could no longer focus on the notation. I did not want to confront the empty bed, made up with lace coverlet and still smelling faintly of gardenia cologne. *It's just a bed*, I told myself. It is of no especial significance, no more than the last fork she'd used, or the last newspaper she'd read.

I slipped into the sheets, pulling the coverlet up to my ears (I suffered from chills at night, when my body temperature plummeted – the result of some inability to regulate temperature). I donned a mask in an attempt to shut out visual distractions. I recited the Latin rite of vespers, hoping that sleep would inevitably overcome me and I could dispel, once and for all, the notion that I was unable to accept Mother's death and the fact that my life, unwound from hers, would continue.

Sicut erat in principio, et nunc et simper, et in saecula saeculorum. As it was in the beginning is now and ever shall be world without end. Amen. I sang the hymns and the psalms as I remembered them from my days in the Burgundian monastery. I sang the Gloria Patri. I sang the Magnificat, and the canticle of the Blessed Virgin Mary from the Gospel of Luke.

Still, sleep eluded me.

Deus, in adiutorium meum intende. Domine, ad adiuvandum me festina.

I had never been feverishly religious. It was simply inevitable that I, as a scholar of Early Music, develop a familiarity with the church offices. Not until the fourteenth century, the era of the troubadour, do we witness significant musical development in the secular sphere. Even then, early motets were composed of phrases co-opted from church music, and not terribly original.

Somehow, the dawn arrived. I remembered fragments of dreams, mostly of Mrs. Hildebrandt. I dreamt that I had wheeled her down a light-flooded corridor, toward a blank white space. (The day previous Mrs. Hildebrandt had been transferred to the nursing home; mental health professionals had attested that she was no longer able to appreciate reality, nor to recognize the surroundings in which she had lived for fifty years, festering and filing excessive noise complaints.) *Faster, faster*, she ordered me. I endeavored to comply, but stumbled over a rubber nub that must have fallen off one of the other residents' walkers, and nearly fell down. *Faster*, she repeated, growing exasperated. Words unfurled across the floor – biblical verses, the canonical mass, the definitive translation of the epic poem Roman de Fauvel. I tried to slow down, to read the messages that had appeared underfoot, but she bade me *faster, faster*, and I stumbled, upending the chair and catapulting Mrs. Hildebrandt toward another dimension.

31.

Shortly after transfer to the Riverview Senior Care Facility, Mrs. Hildebrandt died as the result of a fatal allergic reaction to the filet of sole. An autopsy confirmed that she was allergic to a protein in the fish, an unknown sensitivity Mrs. Hildebrandt, in advanced dementia, had evidently forgot to inform the staff of.

"There will be a service tomorrow." Jose handed me a sheet reciting the particulars of the funereal rites.

I stuffed the leaflet in my jacket pocket and ran upstairs, breathless. Animal rescue services were in the process of removing the orphaned terrier from Mrs. Hildebrandt's apartment. I commiserated with the poor beast – life upended when its owner died precipitously. I gazed at the dimensions of Mrs. Hildebrandt's life. Five hundred square feet, more or less. She had no friends and no living relatives, not even a distant cousin twice removed; anyone with whom she had been acquainted had long ago expired. There was no one to sort through the bric-a-brac, to haul off the extra Dog Chow. By the end of the week, after management had the apartment professionally cleaned, no echo of her would remain.

I could not help but feel that I had somehow willed it to happen, that my animus toward Mrs. Hildebrandt – who interrupted me during practice sessions, throwing off my sense of meter with her relentless pounding against the wall – had been made manifest in the form of a highly sensitive allergy and a largely indifferent nursing staff. Mrs. Hildebrandt died, her airway closing off from acute anaphylactic shock, while her roommate laughed – laughed! – apparently mistaking her for an enthusiastic player of charades.

Oh, why did death seem to follow in my wake? I could not help but feel that I, like one of the fetid pilgrims to the shrine of Lourdes, carried a whiff of the morbid about me.

Blaming Cecilia, insinuating that she was insensitive for enjoying pork gyoza, would not solve anything. She was my most fervent supporter, the one who stood by me as I wallowed in cold potato soup, as I howled piteously in the night, when I awoke, sweating, from nightmares, berating myself for not having done more.

Perhaps it was not too late to recant, to offer a belated apology for my pathological grief abreaction. After all, she had a self-determined right to order take-out from wherever she wanted. I needed Cecilia now. Only she could walk me through this minor tragedy.

"Mrs. Hildebrandt just died," I stammered. "I had a dream about her last night. I was pushing her in a wheelchair down a long corridor, toward the white light. The white light! It was a prophesy," I said, breathless.

Cecilia sighed. She was evidently annoyed that I was pestering her for professional advice after our rupture.

"I'm sorry to trouble you, Cecilia. I'm just in terrible straits. I know I've acted terribly toward you. I know you've had to endure quite enough."

"It's just a coincidence, Luther. Do you think you could will someone to die? That your thoughts are somehow transmitted through the air to the nursing care facility where a demented woman picks them up and acts on them?"

Alas, the relentless "reality testing" of the cognitive behavioral therapist. Pose questions to the analysand in the starkest of terms, making their illogic patent. I hated when she spoke like that, making my feelings seem absurd and the conclusions I drew from objective evidence the irrational ravings of a madman. "Why not?" I countered. "You know I despised the old woman. She knew I despised her. What else could it mean? I was wheeling her toward a white light, for God's sake!"

"Obviously shorthand for the death experience. A modern cliché, deriving from processes attendant to brain death.

"That's my professional opinion," she sniffed. "You've imputed magical powers to yourself to account for the randomness of the universe. Your mother dies in a freak choking accident, then Mrs. Hildebrandt has a fatal allergic reaction to seafood. You think you caused her death because you think you caused your mother's death, and you're continuing to blame yourself because you'd rather believe that you have control over what is essentially beyond your control." She sighed.

By another wretched coincidence, Mrs. Hildebrandt's service took place at M. & Sons Funeral Chapel. I shared a taxi with Jose, who attended as the building's representative. As we approached the sober marble edifice I felt my pulse quicken, my heart palpate, my skin flush. Images of Mother in the Eternal Bronze coffin, hands epoxied around a crucifix ($10 for miscellaneous religious item), flashed in my mind. I knew these to be the symptoms of post-traumatic stress disorder, a perversion of the normal stages of denial, anger, bargaining, depression, the ever-elusive acceptance. Knowing the axis on which to group my dysfunction, however, in no way helped to calm my nerves. Mr. M.'s sons ushered us into the "presentation" room. My legs weakened and buckled underneath me; I could not speak, or even summon a drop of saliva to lubricate my desiccated lips. Jose directed me to a sofa where I might compose myself. I remembered being in Mr. M.'s showroom, selecting from among his wares the casket in which my mother would forever repose in anaerobic darkness. I remembered asking whether we could inter Mother forthwith, without embalming or morbid preparations, but Mr. M. balked, informing me that there were laws of sanitation and decency that prevented him from complying with my wishes. I remembered an awkward conversation about whether or not Mother needed underwear or stockings in her final state of repose, or whether the blue tea-length dress would suffice.

I remained in the rear of the chapel, far from the deceased in the half-open coffin. Everyone remarked that Mrs. Hildebrandt looked rather well: plumper than they had remembered, complexion more robust – no doubt the product of Mr. M.'s diabolical creams and preparations.

A nondenominational chaplain (no one was certain of Mrs. Hildebrandt's religious persuasion) said a few words, inviting us to pray for our dearly departed sister Marguerite.

I noticed Cecilia among the mourners. "Why are you here, Luther?" she asked. Her face was furrowed with concern.

"Why am I here? It seemed only right. She was our neighbor for forty years."

"Mrs. Hildebrandt was only day residue," she said. "A stand in for your mother. You feel responsible for her death, and that's why you dreamed of pushing Mrs. Hildebrandt down the corridor toward the white light."

I supposed I should be thankful for this piece of gratuitous professional insight. Grateful that my girlfriend, or former girlfriend, still cared about my process of grief and was determined to mitigate my guilt through vigorous reality testing.

"You know it wasn't your fault." She touched my arm. "Going to Mrs. Hildebrandt's service, at the very same mortuary, is morbid retroflection. You're trying to reconnect with your mother, but it's not productive. You're simply cementing your negative recollections of this funeral home and aggravating post-traumatic stress." I wondered how it felt having a grief-stricken guinea pig on which to test her accumulated knowledge of the grieving process. An intimate who was experiencing complicated grief in all its physiological and psychological manifestations.

"Let me take you home."

"Fine," I said.

I knelt and said a final prayer. Mrs. Hildebrandt's fingers were interlaced and glued into place. The severe hives that had hastened her demise buried under layers of corrective cosmetics. The final meal evacuated from her body. The blood drained through a discreet incision in the jugular. In the months since Mother's passing I had familiarized myself with the lurid particulars of the death care industry, a morbid fascination Cecilia said was a perverse way of identifying with Mother.

I asked the taxi driver to avoid Third Avenue so I would not have to see the razed lot where Rolf's had once stood.

"I'm sorry that I ejected you from the apartment so precipitously," I said. "I'm dealing with a lot. Not just Mother. Burt has informed me that we can no longer fund the Early Music Symposium." It was the first I had spoken it aloud.

"I'm so sorry, Luther," she said, grabbing my hand, taking into account the compound losses, events that prolonged the healing process and increased the likelihood of *pathological grief.*

"This year's symposium will proceed as scheduled. However, it will be the last one," I said. Did foreknowledge of loss render it any less acute? Did it give you time to acclimate, to absorb the keening blow? Or did it prolong the inevitable feelings of loss?

I would never again convene with my colleagues over mushroom quiches in the foyer of the Tishman Wing. I would miss the mournful timbre of the mother-child virginal, expertly played by Wilhelm Helmutschutter, professor emeritus of musicology at the University of Hamburg.

"Do you want to stop by for a while?" Cecilia asked, plucking the balled-up tissue from my fist.

"Yes," I stammered, my nerves a-jangle. "Are you sure?" I asked. My eyelid trembled. It was a tic I had only recently acquired, as if walking with one foot dragging behind me were not enough to set me apart as a maladroit wreck.

"I'm sure," she replied. I placed my head on her lap, watching the world pass by, inverted, upside down.

Last we had seen one another, we had quarreled over take-out Chinese, splintered chopsticks, the morality of patronizing an establishment that had prepared Mother's final meal. We argued over whether Cecilia's desire for No. 23 (pepper steak) outweighed fealty to Mother; whether standing by me extended to my boycott of Seven Happiness take-away; whether she could support me while still surreptitiously nibbling on their fortune cookies, crumbling oracles I would find between the sofa cushions, *If you don't give something, you will not get anything. Not all closed eye is sleeping, nor open eye seeing.*

She did not allude to the rupture, nor did I. We sat together on the futon in her studio, and had a *digestif.* We spoke not of death, nor of Chinese take-out, but of spring plantings and hyacinth bulbs, of Strauss waltzes and Chopin bagatelles, three fourths time, and bright, major cadences, how we missed one another, her deepest apologies for walking out on me while I was obviously in the midst of pathological grief abreaction.

"I'm sorry, Luther. It was insensitive. I shouldn't have ordered from them, not when you've invested so much emotional weight in the symbolism of the meal. You've displaced so much of the emotional weight of the experience onto the restaurant. Ordering from them must have seemed like a betrayal, an abnegation of your mother's memory and everything you've been through–"

"It's okay. It's all right." I forgave her.

I fell into her arms, and wrestled with her dress, until, finally, I found the knot that unraveled it all. She was still lovely. A little older perhaps, creases visible around her mouth, parenthetical reminders of age, but lovely nonetheless, and I surmised that she, like I, had not had intimate relations for a three-week period. Love, in the end, was an irreducible equation, something beyond our feeble grasp.

"I love you, Cecilia," I whispered in her ear.

"I love you, too, Luther," she said, placing my trembling hand on her breast. "It'll be okay," she assured me, as she stuffed an orthopedic pillow behind my back, and maneuvered on top of me. I noticed that she, too, had lost some weight, albeit likely not from stomach upset and unrelenting, enervating gloom. I was reminded – the firm pressure, the pleasant rhythmic variation, the tonal shadings, like a sonata exploring its theme, *presto vivace* – of the many reasons why I loved her. And why I needed her now: to prop me up with supportive pillows, to massage the cramp in my thigh, to scrub the unreachable, flaking patch of skin on my right shoulder blade, to whisper into my ear, accursed, pitch perfect apparatus, that everything would be all right. She was there for me, willing to renounce pepper steak No. 23 if doing so would restore the harmony of the spheres.

We went to bed, nestled together.

32.

I continued with preparations for the Early Music Symposium. I expected the arrival of several professors of musicology and Renaissance studies, period luthiers and clavier builders, historical theorists, all of us experts on a glorious musical epoch that had been swept aside by those intent on splitting the octave. The majority of the symposium participants came from Italy and the Franco-Flemish lowlands, areas that had been the greatest centers for harpsichord building in the sixteenth and seventeenth centuries. From Fribourg I expected Jacques St. Jacques, a specialist in early schools of organum; from Hamburg, Wilhelm Helmutschutter, Ernst's colleague and critic; from Bruxelles, Yves de Couchet, distant descendant of the harpsichord-making dynasty, who maintained in the family chalet several exemplars of the sixteenth century clavier, as well as instruments whose keyboards and ranges had been extended in the process of *ravalement*, to breathe new life into the instrument and avert the vexing von Blankenburg problem presented by altering the keyboard's disposition.

The opposition of Ernst, professor emeritus at the University of Hamburg, recipient of various chairs and prizes including the Rameau distinguished professor of music and the Santiago de Compostela *bourse*, had energized and united us.

Tonality is not a convenient equidistant construct. Anyone who has heard the *Well-Tempered Clavier* as it was intended to be played, who has appreciated the polyphonic lines of a fourteenth- century motet, can apprehend the truth of this observation: there are heavenly, sonorous tones, auspicious ratios, that have been eliminated in the interest of uniformity.

We had scheduled a practicum on the *Well-Tempered Clavier*, canonical pieces illustrating the aural signatures of various keys within an irregular temperament (E major, bombastic; B-flat major, melancholic, etc.). A reenactment of the grand debates of Zarlino and Galilei, the former an advocate of the mean-tone, the latter an early champion of the equal temperament, a heretical adversary like his son the astronomer. A performance celebrating Nicola Vincentino, inventor of the archicembelo, an instrument capable of replicating all of the sounds in the aural spectrum, without need for retuning or further adjustments.

I could not tell my colleagues that funding for the Early Music Symposium had been eliminated; that this year marked the final one we would gather at the university to toast the latest scholarly dissertation on pre-mensural practice or the margin notes in the Wolfenbüttel Codex; that our period instruments, clavicytheriums, lira da gambas, mother-child virginals, would return from whence they came, never again to commune in sympathetic vibration; that henceforth we would be relegated to our monasteries, our ancient colleges, our Baroque churches, our musty ducal libraries, to author our screeds and codices on ancient tonal systems that could no longer be apprehended.

33.

I had several more dreams, ostensibly about Mrs. Hildebrandt. In them, I was pushing her in a wheelchair, or carrying her awkwardly on my back while she subjected me to a stream of insults. I opened up a book of psalms, intending to recite the *Gloria Patri,* and instead found myself unfolding a takeout menu from Seven Happiness, page upon page of incomprehensible characters, impossible, like a road map, to refold once it had been opened. I dreamed that I received a certificate in food preparation, attesting – like those posted on the premises of Seven Happiness – that I could be trusted to prepare a meal free of bacteriological pathogen associated with food-borne illness. Yet I saw myself blithely deboning sole, and handing it off to the nurse's aide, who would deliver it to Mrs. Hildebrandt in the wing for the memory impaired, a place neither here, nor there, nor anywhere in the cerebro-cortices of its challenged patients, their memories dissolving like the tapioca pudding served with the luncheon menu.

"More guilt dreams," Cecilia pronounced, marveling at my capacity for symbolic association. "You need an immersion session to purge the content from your mind. You need to strip the experience of its associative weight, so that you stop tripping over these emotional minefields.

"If you slept more deeply," Cecilia opined, "you would remember none of it."

I sighed. I never entered stage three or four sleep, the stages in which children slept, oblivious to the world. They could dream of monsters and boogeymen, and remember none of it come the morn, while I, miserable I, remembered every fragment, piecing them obsessively together upon awakening, as if I could ever make sense of the greater symbolic whole.

"What are you doing today?" Cecilia asked.

"Nothing much," I replied. "Preparing for the symposium. A meeting with the custodians of the Fenster Wing concerning transportation of the instruments (they would be hoisted through an old air shaft; coincidentally, the marked escape exit in the event of another protest by the Animal Liberation Organization)."

"It must be difficult," she said, patting my hand, removing a smudge of marmalade from my lip, a smearable substance to be found in fruit baskets and packages of condolences, an *oomph* to the stale, crumbling toast we grief-stricken subsisted on.

"It is," I said. "Piccolo, too, is suffering his usual panic." Despite apprising him in advance of the location of the emergency exits on the plane, despite sending him a useful sheet of exercises to avert Deep Vein Thrombosis – rolling the ankles, lifting the knees, all safely carried out in the seat, under the airplane blanket – he was still worried about the trans-Atlantic crossing, still threatening to remain home in Bologna, not trusting in compression stockings to maintain circulation midair.

"It will be good to be among friends and colleagues," she said.

"Yes, yes," I muttered, licking the marmalade from the far corners of my mouth and the crevices of my teeth.

"Are you sure you'll be okay?" she asked.

She was leaving for the Annual Meeting of the Society of Professional Thanatologists and was not expected to return until the week following.

"Yes, yes. Rest assured," I replied. "I have the strawberry jam, the blueberry jam, the blackberry preserves for the beginning of next week. Some cracked wheat crackers and soft cheeses lurking in a basket I had forgotten about. . . ."

"It's okay," I reiterated. "There's no need to worry."

I'd neglected to tell her that I'd filed a verified complaint seeking damages on account of Mother's precipitous yet utterly preventable demise; that my aversion to Seven Happiness take-out was not merely a phobic reaction, attributable to Mother's death, but the result of express instructions by my counselor-at-law not to frequent the premises; that my deposition was scheduled for Wednesday next, at the offices of Bloodstone & Moore; that my interlocutor, Stewart Cushman, had a reputation for being plodding yet diabolical; that Ms. La Planta had subjected me to hours of simulated cross-examination, hoping to prepare me for the verbal battle, screaming at me to listen to the question asked, to answer only the question asked, and not to volunteer information; that I awoke, sweating, in the middle of the night, dreaming not only of Mrs. Hildebrandt, and my dead Mother, but of interrogation, of being made to recount the particulars of the incident, *She turned blue, the color drained from her, I tried, I tried, to perform the Heimlich maneuver, but I failed, I failed.*

What if the cause of Mother's precipitous demise was not undercooked wontons, or inferior grade lye paste, or an unanticipated tangle of bok choy, as alleged in the verified complaint, but me, inept me, unable to perform basic life-saving maneuvers, *a fist positioned under the rib cage, a thrust delivered decisively upward.*

34.

Ms. La Planta deposed Gary Li, put forth as the "corporate representative" of Seven Happiness. Mr. Li denied that Seven Happiness let deliveries languish for half an hour or more; that it used inferior grade lye paste; that wontons become gelatinous and difficult to chew if not properly prepared. He admitted that on the night of the fatal incident Seven Happiness was understaffed; that the wontons had not been prepared according to the Shanghai style, but to another (one might argue) fatal variation. The deliveryman had since been fired, and deported back to Jiangsu province, where he was apparently beyond the subpoena power of the New York State court system.

Ms. La Planta was heartened by the occurrence of another fatality associated with the Seven Happiness enterprise: apparently, a patron of the West Forty-Seventh Street store had suffered a heart attack, shortly after eating the moo shoo pork. The two incidents were seemingly unconnected, but this latest episode might incline Seven Happiness toward swift settlement so as to avoid the prospect of further negative publicity associated with its take-out operation.

My counselor and I met in the food court, one day prior to my scheduled deposition. "Do you want something to eat?"

Ms. La Planta asked, opening her plastic take-out container. Tuna salad on rye with a pickle spear.

"No thank you," I replied. "I'm not hungry."

"You know, Luther," she continued, chewing five or six times on average before swallowing, rather than the recommended thirty to forty chews per morsel. "I'm just your attorney. I'm here to defend your legal rights, to see you vindicated in the courts of justice. To negotiate, at the very least, a generous settlement from their insurance carrier." She wiped the mayonnaise delicately from her mouth with a napkin. "But nothing I do can bring your mother back. That's a loss you have to deal with." I pondered the many, exponential ways in which food could become stuck in the windpipe (failure of the epiglottis to seal, failure of the nasopharynx to close off, a defect in one of the numerous muscles that controlled swallowing).

I looked around me: Mongolian Noodle, Fried-Rice Paradise, Churrasco City. India-on-a-plate, Kebab-on-the-go. Squashed cardboard boxes, plastic, see-through containers, chopsticks and plastic utensils that snapped under pressure.

"Are you okay?" Ms. La Planta asked. She placed her manicured nails on my arm.

"I'm all right," I assured her. "The spore index is at an all-time high," I sniffled. I had not slept in days. My dreams kept me awake at night, scenes in which I folded and refolded take-out menus, or was chased by faceless stick figures, the orange and blue ones on the public service announcement for rendering aid to a choking victim, *fist here, pressure up*, all explained in simple pictographs.

"I know it's very stressful," she said. "I've been through this many times," she assured me. "It's normal for clients to be nervous. But I'll be sitting right by your side. I'll object if he crosses the line."

Would there ever be a time when I could recall the memory as if through a haze, rather than imagining it in all its agonizing detail – chest compression, rescue breath, *breathe, breathe* (insistent, intrusive imagery, often interfering with daily functioning, *see* Complicated Grief, Weide *et al.*)?

Ms. La Planta assured me than an offer would be forthcoming once I had been deposed. "It's just the way things work," she informed me. "They're waiting to hear what you have to say before we talk settlement. Just remember to relax," she counseled me, "and take a Xanax half an hour before."

The morning next, I bid *adieu* to Cecilia. "Have fun!" I said. The program (I had stolen a glimpse at the week's schedule) included Working through Denial: How to Acknowledge What Will Not be Acknowledged; Hop-stopping Among the Stages of Grief: Grief is Not Linear; Funeral Homes: Everything You Always Wanted to Know but Were Afraid to Ask (disclaimer: the particulars may be disturbing).

"Are you sure you'll be all right?" she asked, standing curbside.

"I'll be fine," I said. "Don't worry about me." I waved my arms so as to attract the attention of a taxi.

"She's going to Penn Station," I said, throwing her suitcase in the trunk. I stared into the empty black coffer.

"I can cancel if you want."

"No, no, it's not necessary," I assured her, closing the door. I heard the crepitus lurch of the taxi. It turned round the corner, and disappeared from view.

35.

I played Aveline in the middle of the night, in defiance of the rules of the cooperative association. Who would complain, now that Mrs. Hildebrandt was gone? Her apartment was empty and on the market for a sum commensurate to its market value, not the pittance set by the rent control board. I played *Byrd one brere*, an old English love song: *I am so blithe, so bright, bird on a briar/ When I see that handmaid in the hall/ She is white of limb, lovely, true/ She is fair and flower of all.* It was one of Mother's favorites. A simple melody, a triple meter. I could see Mother on the sofa, legs crossed at the ankles, sipping tea from Wedgewood china. She sang along, in a warbly alto-soprano, *Yhe is fayr and flur of alle.*

It was not Machaut, *Se Vous N'Estes*, or *Qui es promesse— Ha! Fortune*, an isorhythmic motet dealing with themes of fate and cosmic justice ("Without faith . . . it's excrement covered with rich covering, which gleams without and within is ordure"). It was a simple love song, a simple image ("bird on a briar"), a universal sentiment ("love thus craves"). Love instills the fear of its loss. The absence of affection, when all is desolate, and love, inverted, becomes howling pain:

Blissful bird, have mercy on me
Or dig, love, dig thou for me my grave.

The morning of the deposition I was seized by an impulse to run off, to flee to an obscure ducal library on the Continent without vindicating my legal rights. I paced about the apartment. I did my best to make myself look presentable, but my cowlick would not be tamed and my overactive sebaceous glands had caused multiple, pustulent eruptions. I brushed my teeth several times but still felt as if something had died within my oral cavity, so resilient was my breath to the artificial peppermint flavoring of my usual toothpaste. I felt the sweat trickling from my armpits and coursing down my sides, worsening the itch of my sweater vest. I sank on the crushed velvet of the bishop's chair, attempting to steady myself, for the world appeared to have veered off course, to be spinning uncontrollably, off its axis. I felt as if I were a celestial body that had been knocked out of orbit.

I was shaken from my disequilibrium by Jose, who had used his spare key to allow Ms. La Planta into the apartment. She had been buzzing me for over ten minutes.

She watched while I choked down an anti-anxiety pill. "We can reschedule," she said.

"No," I insisted. "I want to get it over with."

Though I was familiar with the dimensions of the conference room – the long mahogany table, the row of windows overlooking Forty-Second Street from a calamitous height – I felt as if I had lost my bearings. I sat at the head of the table as directed by the court reporter. I placed my folded hands on the conference room table, in a position suggestive of sober reflection, as I had been counseled by my attorney-at-law.

My inquisitor wore a rumpled navy suit and carried with him a battered leather bag in which I glimpsed several carefully-tabbed file folders. He had giant bearish hands, stubby fingers and a meager finger span – entirely inappropriate for playing a sensitive keyboard or string instrument. The only possible choice for such hands was a brass instrument like a tuba or trombone – assuming he had the embouchure.

He introduced himself ("Stewart Cushman, Stewart Cushman, P.C., it's a pleasure to meet you") and asked if I would like a refreshment, a pathetic attempt to establish rapport with the subject of his questioning. I politely declined, maintaining my hands firmly clasped on the table. He explained the "ground rules" of the deposition, which the court reporter dutifully transcribed:

Please respond verbally. The court reporter cannot transcribe nods or shakes, grunts or groans, [unintelligible].

Please answer the question asked, and only the question asked, or your answers will be [stricken].

Your attorney may object to my questions. You are still obliged to respond.

Speak up, keep your voice UP, so the court report can hear you [click, click, clickety-clack]. You will have a chance to review your transcript afterward and to correct any errors.

Do you swear to tell the truth, the whole truth, and nothing but the truth, so help you God?

"Had you eaten take-out from Seven Happiness before the incident in question?"

"Yes," I replied.

"Approximately how many times?"

"I'm not sure. It would be difficult to estimate."

"More times than you can remember?"

"I don't know. I suppose."

"And on these prior instances you experienced no difficulties chewing the food or otherwise?"

"I did not choke, if that's what you're asking." My counselor-at-law glared at me.

"Had you heard complaints about Seven Happiness from the neighbors?"

"No."

"Have you been deposed before?" he asked. My interlocutor scribbled on his legal pad. He was left-handed. He grasped his pencil with his entire fist, a poor habit of penmanship I had remarked upon in others with the same proclivity. In the Middle Ages he would have been decreed an apprentice of the devil.

"No."

"Have you sued anyone before alleging negligence, recklessness, or the absence of due care, in food preparation or otherwise?"

"No." I responded. Ms. La Planta had warned me that he would try to paint me as a litigious crusader, a blame-shifter, someone who perceived wrongdoing where there was only accidental mishap and unforeseeable circumstance.

"Did your mother have any neurological deficits?"

"No."

"Did she ever have a stroke?"

"No."

"Did she suffer from Parkinson's or other disease affecting control of the muscles?"

"No."

"Did she take any medications?"

"Nothing, other than the occasional aspirin."

"When was the last time she had a medical check-up prior to the incident?"

"Within the preceding year, I would imagine."

"But you don't know for sure?"

"No."

"When was the last time she had a dental check-up?"

"A few months before."

"Were X-rays taken?"

"I believe so."

"We don't have the dental records," he turned to his adversary. "I hereby call for the production of decedent's dental records, including any X-rays and molds. Who was her dentist?"

"Dr. Wong-Goldman, Madison Avenue and Fifty-Fifth." I coughed and asked for a glass of water. Ms. La Planta had warned me about sustained periods of questions and answers in which I could become swept up, forget that Mr. Cushman was a trained inquisitor whose intent was to demolish my veracity and reduce the settlement value of the case, not a friend with whom I was having a congenial chat.

"Did your mother have all of her teeth?"

"Yes."

"Did she have any crowns or implants?"

"No."

"Did she have difficulties masticating her food?"

"No," I scoffed.

"Are you her only relative?" he asked, turning to a new subject.

"Yes, I am her only child."

"Is your father deceased?"

"Yes, in a manner of speaking."

"What does that mean?" he scowled.

"He was declared dead after seven years of continuous absence." I remembered the day Mother received the official declaration, enabling her to assert that she was a widow and the rightful recipient of his social security benefits, not a woman abandoned by a peripatetic dilettante. She said that Father was now deceased, in the eyes of the law, as if having a father who was presumed dead was a happier circumstance than having one who had simply abandoned you, as if the reason you were fatherless could in any way change the mechanism of loss and longing.

"Is there any chance that he can claim the inheritance?"

"I suppose a theoretical one," I responded, the same way there was a theoretical possibility that the Pythagorean ratios could be reconciled, but it would never be.

"Presumed dead is presumed dead," Ms. La Planta interjected. "Let's move on."

"Who ordered the wonton soup?"

"No one. It came with Mother's meal."

"Nonetheless, it was included as a first course with the General Tso chicken."

"Yes. As I understand the menu. Choice of wonton soup or spring roll, choice of entrée, fortune cookie."

"So there was a choice of appetizer?"

"Yes."

"And your mother chose the wonton soup, rather than the spring roll?"

"I suppose."

"Would you agree that spring rolls, which contain chopped pork and vegetables, are more easily masticated than wonton soup, which contains a combination of leafy vegetable and pork dumpling in a hot broth?"

"Objection – what is he, an expert on chewing and swallowing? Move on."

I resented the insinuation that had I been more vigilant I would have realized the danger lurking in the soup – bok choy, a large-leafed, bitter green; wontons, known to become gelatinous under certain conditions. That a spring roll – steamed, with uniformly chopped fillings – was a safer choice? That she would not have died had I more wisely selected?

I heard Contrapunctus VIII, from *The Art of the Fugue*, inside my head. My fingers, conditioned from hours of practice upon the harpsichord, began playing the lines. Left hand swarmed across the conference room table, right hand echoing the pattern, the two in a call-and-answer, figure and recapitulation.

"Who opened the soup container?"

"I believe I did. I unpacked the delivery."

"What was the temperature of the soup?"

"It was warm," I replied. "Not too hot."

"Did your mother burn her tongue?"

"No. I just said the soup was not too hot."

"How do you know? Did you eat it?"

"No, but I tested a spoonful." Mother's teeth were sensitive to temperature extremes, a problem she had remarked upon to Dr. Wong-Goldman.

"How long was she eating before you noticed something was wrong?"

"I don't know. A few minutes."

"Was she sipping broth, eating wontons, or a combination thereof?"

"I believe she was eating a wonton."

"How can you be sure?"

"She was chewing." I saw her jaw muscles working, her mouth purse in recognition of the bitterness of the bok choy, a vegetable she was not fond of. Did the leafy green catch her unawares? Was the wonton impossible to masticate? In the ordinary course of events, she would have deposited difficult-to-chew items on the edge of her plate. I remember seeing a lump in her throat, realizing that the wonton had become stuck. Transitional chords, enharmonic spellings that could resolve one way or the other – cadence in the major as expected, or take a turn into a darker, minor key. I believed, like I believed on the innumerable prior occasions I had shared supper with her and something had gone down the wrong way – that the situation would resolve on its own in a fit of coughing or chest pounding. But instead, the wonton insinuated itself in her throat, and there was only the silence of *total airway obstruction.*

"How many times did she chew the wonton?"

"I don't know. Enough to break it up."

"Move to strike as nonresponsive. Do you in fact know how many times she chewed the wonton?"

"No."

"What happened next?"

"I noticed she was gagging. I asked if she wanted a drink of water. At that point I thought something had just gone down the wrong way."

"Did she indicate that she wanted water?"

"No, but it was evident to me that something had become stuck in her throat."

"How can you be sure?"

"Because she opened her mouth, as if to say something, but no words escaped."

"Please continue."

"She placed her hands around her throat, indicating to me that she was choking."

"What type of gesture, exactly?"

I placed my hands around my neck.

"Let the record reflect that the witness is encircling the neck with both hands, fingers interlaced at the level of the voice box. What did this gesture signify to you?"

"That she was choking, of course."

I had seen the public service announcements, conspicuously posted in take-out establishments, depicting a slumped-over victim and her would-be rescuer – double fist positioned halfway between naval and sternum, the exhortation to *drive upward with great force*, which would cause the choking victim to expel the wily chicken bone or popcorn kernel that had become stuck in her throat. *Ask the victim if he/she is choking. If he/she is choking, he/she will be unable to respond. Even a high whine or wheeze indicates that the airway is not totally blocked and is an encouraging sign. Another reliable indicator of airway obstruction is the "universal sign for choking" – placement of two hands around the neck.*

"What did you do?"

"I leapt up, stood behind Mother, and attempted to perform the Heimlich maneuver."

"By Heimlich maneuver you mean the maneuver described by Heimlich for emergency evacuation of foreign bodies in the airway, namely, the application of force at the diaphragm?"

"That is what I mean."

"Okay. Go on."

"I drove my fist into her abdomen, but nothing happened. I tried again, but nothing." I performed my part, the call, the melodic gesture, but there was no response, no cough or sputter, no violent expulsion, no percussive *pop*. I imagined the notes she would sound were she uncorked, the shimmering frequencies of her alto-soprano range, the careful distinctions she made between the chromatic and the diatonic semi-tone, in deference to her son the scholar of medieval and Renaissance music.

"Did she cough or gasp at any time while you were performing the Heimlich?"

"No."

"How did she respond, if at all?"

"She didn't respond. The color drained from her face." I remembered the pallor. How quickly the body, deprived of oxygenated blood, grows cold and unresponsive.

I placed my hands on the table. I heard the tapping of the court reporter, transcribing my thoughts in staccato bursts. Riffling through the paper tape to see where she had left off.

"Was she conscious?"

"Most definitely." Ms. La Planta had warned me that damages were only recoverable for conscious pain and suffering; harm visited upon an unconscious victim, no matter how despicable, was without recourse in the law.

"How can you be sure?"

"She was desperately trying to say something. Her eyes pleading with me. She made the universal gesture for choking."

"How long did this go on for?"

"I don't know. It seemed like forever." In moments of trauma, the brain perceives the world in slow motion; everything plays out in a tortuous frame-by-frame. Mother falling to her knees. My feeble attempts at the Heimlich. Prying her mouth open, peering into the convulsing throat, trying to extricate the wonton, so deeply insinuated it was beyond reach.

"How long was she choking before you called 911?"

"I don't know. Thirty seconds."

"Well, 911 records show that you called at 8:53 p.m., and that when a crew arrived at 8:58 p.m. your mother was already in full cardiopulmonary arrest. That's an interval of (he counted on his stubby fingers) five minutes, is it not?"

"The record speaks for itself counselor," Ms. La Planta interjected. "Move on."

"Did you continue your resuscitation efforts after you called 911?"

"Yes." I drove my fist into her stomach. I beseeched the heavens. I made absurd bargains with a God I had known primarily through early church music, inspiration for centuries' worth of plainchant and polyphonic masterpieces, basso pro-fundo intoning Amen while the upper voices soared. *Save her, I said to him. She is only sixty-two. She has three years left as president of the New York City chapter of the Richard Wagner Society. She is the only relative I have ever known. I would be lost without her.* This was a prayer, as much as the Gloria Patri or Magnificat. Would the chord resolve harmoniously, in one of the usable keys in the quarter-comma meantone? Or would it veer into a key with a howling "wolfe" interval, an abomi-nation instrument makers avoided rather than confront, un-able to eliminate this sour possibility from the aural spectrum? Alas, it was to be the latter. After another soundless cough, she closed her eyes, and the spirit left her.

The overtone series is the best evidence we have of the true and intended musical proportions. The aural compromises de-manded by the equal temperament revealed to be nothing but a dissonant sham. Only if a string is precisely tuned, according to the true Pythagorean proportions, will its overtones series – fifth, fourth and so on – beat in perfect consonance.

"What happened when the ambulance crew arrived?" Mr. Cushman asked, pouring himself a glass of water.

"Jose let them in. They rushed into the apartment. One of them shone a light into her eyes. The other listened to her heart with a stethoscope, shook his head. 'I'm not registering any-thing,' he said. He unbuttoned her blouse (forgive me Mother! but the dead have no right of privacy), placed the paddles over her chest. 'There's no electrical activity.'" *No electrical activity.* I struggled to remain still, not to cry out to the heavens, not to weep on the inlaid mahogany table, not to shred the legal pad Ms. La Planta had given me so I would have something upon which to doodle, *Notes on a Deposition*, *A Caprice in E-Flat*. This divertimento was my Mother's life, or at least the last five recorded minutes of it, the cadence, the final bars, the *fermata*, an indefinite suspension.

"Do you need to take a break?" Ms. La Planta interjected. Even she, with her deposition simulation, her mock cross-examination, had not prepared me for this brutal dissection of Mother's character, the insinuations of excessive alcohol consumption and poor dentition, the insistence on recounting the incident in all of its agonizing particulars, *She turned blue, I mean ashen, waxen*, making me revisit the final, decisive moments of Mother's life, to attest to my deficient life-saving technique and my inability to perform the Heimlich maneuver, hoping to seize on some inconsequential inconsistency, something he could exploit, highlight on the transcript in medium yellow marker. Oh, Mother! Even if I were to win some small pittance, to settle the case for what Ms. La Planta called "nuisance value," nothing could bring her back.

"No." I waved my attorney off. "Let's press on."

"At what point during this incident did your mother officially die?"

"I believe that's a question for the medical examiner." Ms. La Planta interjected.

"At what point did you believe her to be dead?"

"OBJECTION, argumentative."

"It's a fair question."

"I suspected she was dead, but I did not learn until afterwards, at the hospital, that she had passed." My fingers, tightly interlaced, began trembling. In my heart, I had known she was dead. There was no doubt that *lack of electrical activity, only the faintest, detectable pulse*, was paramedic code for *no chance of survival*. Yet so long as I did not utter the words, so long as I could blithely follow the ambulance to the hospital, fill out the clipboarded paperwork, utilizing the dangling pen affixed thereto, a cheap stylus that globbed up on the page as I was trying helpfully to fill in date of birth and relevant medical history, *hypertension, diabetes, no, no, no*, I could pretend that she was still alive, that she was being admitted to the hospital, rather than re-routed to the morgue. Oh, Mother! So long as I refused to utter the words, to press hospital staff about Mother's condition, *no word, no confirmation, not authorized at this time to say anything*, I could continue to believe that she was alive, that I would sign the discharge papers authorizing her release, chide her for swallowing before chewing, crack open our fortune cookies.

Someday everything will all make sense.

"Who told you that your mother had died?"

I riffled through memory. "A nurse, I believe." I had forgotten this detail. "She emerged from the room where they had been 'working on her.' She said, 'I'm so sorry. There was nothing to be done.'" Nothing to be done. No one ever actually said *your mother is dead*. The hospital social worker arrived several minutes later, inquiring whether there was anyone she could call on my behalf. She telephoned Cecilia and recounted the sordid tale, *Yes, umm, well, she asphyxiated while eating wonton soup, tragic, um*; minutes later, Cecilia arrived, searching around frantically, *Where can I find Mr. van der Loon?* It was not until I saw the measure of sadness in her eyes, mirroring the tragic circumstances, that I broke down, weeping in the corridor. A howl that resonates in my nightmares, a blank white echo. At the end of the hallway there is nothing, nothing but an empty circle of light.

"Was an autopsy performed?" Mr. Cushman inquired.

"Yes," I replied.

"And what were the results of the autopsy?"

"OBJECTION. The report speaks for itself. You can read as well as I."

"Very well. He opened his briefcase and removed therefrom a manila folder containing copies of the AUTOPSY REPORT.

"I will read from the preamble. Cause of death: FBAO, foreign body airway obstruction attendant to incomplete aspiration of food bolus." He looked over his half-glasses, directly at me. "Now I ask you. You can read the report yourself. Does it say anything about gelatinous lye paste, or tangled bok choy, or any of the other colorful descriptors you employ in your verified complaint seeking damages on account of your mother's death?"

"OBJECTION. Don't answer that," my counselor-at-law instructed me.

"It does not, I assure you," he continued. "I've read it several times, and no such descriptions are to be found. Indeed, examination under microscope showed the FB to be partially masticated dough, nothing more, nothing less."

"Stop harassing my client and get on with it." Ms. La Planta drummed her nails on the conference room table. "Are you almost finished? It's nearly lunchtime."

"Please read back the question," Mr. Cushman directed the court reporter, stuffing his face with a cheese Danish.

"Does it say. . ." The paper spilled onto the floor from the stenography machine, page upon page of impressions and ruts and hole-punched exchanges. "Does it say anything about," she paused, squinting at one of the passages. "Gelatin. . ."

"Gelatinous."

"Gelatinous lye paste . . ."

"That's enough, Stewart. I'm directing him not to answer," my counselor-at-law shot back.

"Fine."

"Are you done?" my lawyer asked.

"For now. But I reserve the right to recall the witness for further questioning."

36.

Cecilia returned from the Annual Meeting of the Society of Thanatologists the following week, feeling rejuvenated.

"They're going to recognize us as a separate chapter," she glowed. "Specialists in traumatic bereavement."

"That's wonderful, darling." I slathered marmalade on a piece of crustless toast, some *oomph* to the stale bread.

"I wish you could have been there, Luther. The support group is really a wonderful forum for expressing grief and enlisting the empathy of fellow survivors. It's not all babbling and group cries, you know?"

"I know, Cecilia." Indeed, it was unburdening of the most hideous kind: awful revelations, obscene medical details (His blood oxygen level was down to 40% before he started gasping for air!, She was oozing out of every orifice, no matter how much gauze I stuffed in there!). Your overwhelming sense of guilt, of incapacity, of helplessness (I can't detect a pulse!) somehow comforting to your fellow group members, making them feel as if they had done all they could.

"I led a group whose loved ones had succumbed to cancer. It was cleansing for all of us." What did they know of my pain – they who at least had some forewarning, the courtesy of a diagnosis, some reasonable approximation of life expectancy?

Their loved ones could make the most of the time remaining. They could compose letters to the survivors (*What I've learned from life is. . . .*). They could go on seaside holiday, frolic in the waves one last time. What did they know of foreign body airway obstruction? Of lye paste and smashed fortunes?

"I'm really very happy for you, darling. Opportunities for professional growth and all." I unscrewed the jar of blackberry preserves. My last consolation prize.

"How long can you go on, eating toast and puréed foods?" Cecilia asked. "You need some protein. You're looking anemic again."

If I wanted to subsist on bread and preserves, if I wanted to run food through a blender on high speed, meals suitable for a toothless, demented old woman with a swallowing dis-order – so what?

"Why don't we order in?" she suggested.

"I can't."

"You're not dishonoring your mother by ordering Chinese take-out from the place that happened to prepare her last meal."

"No," I insisted, though of late I had missed the beef and broccoli (four red peppers out of a possible five), the sesame chicken, with its glazed orange sheen (five out of five peppers, spicy hot), the chow fun, thick noodles teeming in a shallow broth (two out of five peppers, not particularly spicy).

"Luther, this is a big stumbling block for you. You can't fetishize Chinese take-out, ascribing it magical properties, just because it was part of the stage of your mother's death. There's nothing inherently evil about wonton soup."

"Really, Cecilia?" I fumed. I struggled to spread an even layer of preserves on my toast.

"Why don't we just try it?" she softened. "We can order the lunch special. . ."

"You won't find a menu in the house," I shot back. I had confiscated all of them.

"It's okay. I remember the menu. Let's just call." She picked up the telephone, punched in a number, started to speak – *I'd like to place an order. Can I get the lunch special? Yes, with spring roll* – when I snatched the receiver from her hand and terminated the call.

"Luther, what are you doing?"

"I can't let you order from them,"

"I know it's difficult, but–"

"I can't." I protested. I sank into the gothic bishop's chair. The room swirled around me. Though everywhere I saw the artifacts of Mother's life – the embroidered pillows, the commemorative beer stein, the quaint charcoals of Zugspitze, the "Matterhorn" of Bavaria – she was no longer there. There was a cosmic dissonance. Facts I could not accept as having transpired –- *viz.*, she choked on a wonton, the autopsy confirms it; the Eternal Bronze is the top-of-the-line in eternal luxury. I blinked, several times in succession, as if I had just awoken from a bad dream and was waiting for the world to readjust. But this was reality, not a dream; this was the waking world, in all its cold, bleak detail. (I was looking peaked, absolutely peaked, as Cecilia had said, fearful of swallowing my iron supplement – a horse pill if ever there was one.) An empty sofa and a hollow tea cup, faded watercolors of the Bavarian countryside, the white-and-blue escutcheon. If only I had been there for the Beer Hall Putsch of 1923, if only Mother were here now, eating Seven Happiness Chinese take-out, No. 23 General Tso chicken, as if none of it had ever happened. An alternate ending, *da capo*, back to the beginning.

"Luther, are you all right?" She placed a hand on my arm.

"It's just a dizzy spell," I said, gripping the arm rests.

"You can do this, Luther. I'll walk you through it." She wiped the sweat from my brow. Of late, it seemed like my essence was seeping from me, as if I would drown in a sea of lachrymose secretions. "Let's open the window," she suggested.

"No," I said, trying to steady myself, to stand up, but my knees buckled underneath me.

"Luther, what is it?" she searched my eyes (my crusty, red, itchy, tear-duct clogged eyes).

It seemed, in the months following Mother's death, as if I were living in a state of indefinite suspension. Would I recover, learn to assimilate grievous loss? Would events, like a piece in a minor key that in the final bars veers into the major – the Piccadilly third, a popular cadence in the late Renaissance – take a turn for the better? Or would it end, inevitably, in a minor key?

"Luther, what is it?" she asked.

"Cecilia, there's something I need to tell you," I said, avoiding her gaze, the therapeutic eye lock said to be conducive to unburdening and un-self-conscious revelation.

"Tell me," she implored.

"Very well," I said, folding my hands on the table. "I've sued the Seven Happiness franchise and Bernice Wong, individually, for negligence and carelessness in food preparation." I took a deep breath.

And here I unburdened myself thoroughly. I told Cecilia about my deposition the week previous, about my interlocutor, Mr. Cushman, Stewart Cushman, P.C., offices in White Plains and Garden City, Long Island. I told of his dogged questioning; of his fat-knuckled brio; of his insinuations, beyond the bounds of acceptable advocacy, that Mother's poor dentition and alcohol intake contributed to her hasty demise. I told of his cramped, left-handed penmanship, filling page upon page of yellow legal paper; of his eyes, obscured by thick corrective lenses; of his habit of lip smacking; of the Danish flake that was poised on his lip for what seemed like hours while he pounded away, questioning my recollection of events, *How can you be certain that she choked on a wonton? How long before she turned blue? Did you attempt to perform the Heimlich maneuver?, When was she pronounced deceased?*; of the hours of interrogation, punctuated only by the tap-tap-tap of the court reporter's machine, the occasional OBJECTION of my counselor-at-law. We fell into a pattern, call-response, theme-variation: *You'd never had a complaint with Seven Happiness previously, had you?* (No, their food was quite tasty), *In fact, you ordered from Seven Happiness take-out four times a week, on average, didn't you?* (General Tso on Tuesdays, sesame noodles on Wednesday, Sichuan fried rice on Thursday. . .), *Did you peer inside your mother's throat?* (Yes, yes, [sob], it was spasming), *Did you see the foreign object?* (Yes, peering inside a dark passage). The rules of counterpoint dictate that voices should move in opposite directions, together and apart. Mother had died before my eyes, fallen to her knees with her hands around the throat; she had faded, passed into obscurity, in the span it took to separate my chopsticks. There one moment, gone the next, a truncated musical passage: gone, gone, gone.

"Oh, Luther." She squeezed my hand, a bit too tightly.

"The joints," I winced. "So you see, I cannot step foot in Seven Happiness Chinese take-out. In any event, they refuse to deliver here, claiming that I've unfairly denigrated their take-out enterprise."

"Is that why Jose's been going there to pick up orders?"

I blushed. "I'm under strict instructions to boycott the franchise, lest I compromise my position in ongoing settlement negotiations." My hands fell into my lap. Gnarled, permanently curled, the recommended position for optimal keyboard attack. The harpsichordist is urged to strive for precision in execution of difficult musical passages. He must convey the emotional nuances of a work through deft fingerwork and delicate phrasing, lacking the sustain pedal and showy dynamics of the piano.

"What are your chances?"

"My attorney hopes to settle the case for what she calls 'nuisance value' [i.e., what others will pay to silence you, and be done with it, rather than financing the ongoing costs of litigation]. Our chances significantly diminish if we go to trial. Negligence in food preparation is a difficult case to prove." I coughed, throat parched.

She, like I, would be forever banished from Seven Happiness, never again to eat shredded beef (five peppers out of a possible five) or Peking duck (three peppers), never again to unfurl the crumpled messages of fortune cookies.

Someday everything will all make sense.

"Well, what's done is done," she sighed.

For the first time since I had commenced the lawsuit, since I had authorized Ms. La Planta to institute an action on my behalf seeking damages for the fallout – I felt relieved, at peace. I had done all I could. It was time to let go, to allow the justice system (*viz.*, the backroom settlement negotiations of Ms. La Planta and Stewart Cushman, P.C.) to run its course. It was time to accept that I, and the entirety of medieval/Renaissance music, had been relegated to the Fenster Wing. It was time to acknowledge that I would never again sip tea with Mother from a cracked china cup, nor regale her with *Byrd one brere*. I had to accept that she was gone, a chord that had finally resolved.

I ripped Cecilia's clothes off, tossed them on the floor, kissing her gently on the underlip. I proceeded, via trilling kisses, through the thick undergrowth – feeling the pulsations, the spasming thigh muscles – until the waves passed, *agitato*, *diminuendo*, and we folded into one another.

37.

Piccolo Fabrizzi took the midnight plane from Bologna, connecting through Schiphol, Amsterdam. After landing at John F. Kennedy airport, he spent an agonizing one-and-a-half hour on the line for nonresidents, having his credentials scrutinized by immigration officials and his baggage searched by an agent apparently unfamiliar with the implements of the luthier's trade, thinking them the burglar's tools of a criminally-minded foreigner, rather than the harmless trinkets of a professor of medieval and Renaissance music.

He informed the taxi dispatcher that he was going to Tudor City. The driver, misapprehending him, deposited him on the west side in the area colloquially known as Hell's Kitchen. By this time the prospect of clot formation was dire, all the moreso because Piccolo had been unable, during his lengthy interrogation and detention by customs, to manage more than a few sips from a mercurial water fountain. He called me, panting and breathless, from the corner of Eighth Avenue and Thirty-Eighth Street, where he had managed to walk though laden awkwardly with lute case and a battered valise that threatened to roll over each time it hit a sidewalk crack.

"I need you to come and get me, my friend," he sputtered.

I hailed a taxi and hastened to the west side. I spotted him on the corner, leaning perilously to one side. Years of lute playing had made him stoop shouldered and caused him to heavily favor the right, so as to keep his head from hitting the extravagantly curved fretboard.

"Piccolo!" I shouted. I placed his baggage in the trunk and instructed the driver to return home. Piccolo was pale and clammy and feeling faint. He gulped down the bottle of spring water I had brought to revive him. "I'm so sorry for your travails, my friend."

"I have a terrible cramp," he said, pointing to his right calf. The trouser leg had been rolled up, revealing the ribbed sock he wore to help with circulation. "This sock, it is useless," he groaned.

Piccolo and I met while I was doing graduate studies on the Continent. He had been instrumental in tracking down for me an obscure volume from the library of the Duchy of Wolfenbüttel, which, by dint of centuries and corrupt deal-making, had found its way into the hands of an eccentric Italian collector. The collector allowed me to view the codex under the fanatical temperature control settings of its room in his villa, a chamber designed to withstand the Tuscany heat and the exhalations of whatever modern-day musicologist dared to turn the manuscript's pages. I took careful, precise notes in my leather-bound notebook, notes which profoundly informed my doctoral thesis on *Pre-Mensural Notation in the Late Fourteenth Century*. The following year, the collector suffered a coronary and his estate was divided by feuding distant relations to whom the codex was but a brittle manuscript in a dead tongue the value of which was not apparent.

Piccolo's circulatory problems had persisted for decades and were relieved only by vigorous manipulation and precisely-applied acupressure points. I put his leg on my lap, rolled down his sock, and began massaging his calf. It was spasmodic and rock hard. Tension that was difficult to break up, despite the finger strength I had acquired as a virtuoso of the harpsichord.

"Relax, my friend," I counseled him. He had an awkward gait, making him seem forever tipsy, though he rebuffed all alcoholic refreshment save for a glass of *Grand Marnier* at bedtime.

Jose greeted us curbside. He tended to Piccolo while I paid the driver and evacuated the luggage from the trunk. The lute needed forthwith to be placed in a cool, dark area so as to prevent warping of its ludicrously arched neck. I thanked Jose for his efforts and told him I could handle it from there. The ascent to the eighth floor caused Piccolo to swoon and cling to the brass elevator railing.

"I will have a drink," Piccolo announced, departing from his usual custom.

He sat in the bishop's chair, gripping both arms, while I fetched his refreshment. I had a bottle of absinthe from Mother's last journey to the Continent. I hesitated to squander the spirits, but wondered what I was holding onto, what I could possibly divine in its vapors that had not already been irreparably, indubitably lost.

"*Salut*," I said.

Piccolo's experience with wormwood liquors was limited. "My friend, I am facing extinction at the University of Bologna," he lamented, choking down the absinthe. "The department is not so popular these days. There is no interest in the study of medieval music." The Renaissance era could at least lay claim to polyphonic textures, early secular music, and instrumental parodies. Medieval music could be summed up in a chapter on responsorials.

"I am tired of this lute-playing for tourists," he groaned, referring to his job serenading restaurant patrons with lute arrangements of popular songs. "It's not good for the circulation. They expect me to stand and to stroll around like a wandering minstrel."

I stared into the glass of absinthe. It was already having an effect. In my haste to retrieve Piccolo I had forgotten to eat. My stomach gnawed at me, sending up acid flares. I had nothing in the apartment save some crusts of bread and an odious blackberry jam, one of many such jars that had appeared on my doorstep in the days following Mother's death, condolences in the form of orange marmalade and strawberry preserves and other smearable substances.

"Alas my friend, the modern world has rendered most of what we do useless," I commiserated. I offered him a slice of bread with blackberry jam, which he declined, citing stomach upset occasioned by the haphazard trans-Atlantic journey. The jar had been left by Mrs. Hildebrandt, who had been fond of my mother, albeit not of me. She had ventured from her agoraphobe's apartment to deposit the jar on the doorstep, with a shaky note and a promise that nuns in the Spanish highlands were saying rosaries in Mother's honor. Celeste, *Sicut erat in principio, et nunc et simper, et in saecula saeculorum,* as it was in the beginning, world without end, Amen. The woman's Latin was perfect, though her synapses could not transmit a coherent thought such as *One cannot live on a diet of canned peaches. Stop banging on the walls and the floors. You're disturbing the neighbors.*

"Medieval music is a thankless field of study," Piccolo sighed. The typical professor of period music had difficulty confronting the modern world. He found comfort in the arched neck of a lute or the dynamically limited keyboard of the harpsichord. He fretted over the difference between a Just third and the Pythagorean tuning; he stayed up nights, restless, thinking up retorts to those who believed equal division of the octave, with its obliteration of the sacred ratios, to be the solution to the "wolfe" tones lurking in the circle of fifths. He was embroiled in the controversies of centuries past, a relic whose identification with figures like Zarlino or Ramos de Pareja – as opposed to musical godheads like Beethoven or Bach – was viewed as perverse.

"What is one to do?" Piccolo sighed. He rotated one ankle, then the other, still concerned about the possibility of blood clots.

"I don't know," I sighed.

I brushed vigorously. I gargled, and spent a long while flossing between second and third molars. I had skipped my annual appointment with Dr. Wong-Goldman, unable to inform her of Mother's passing, still harboring ill feelings towards her for Mother's "poor dentition." Finally, I turned in. I swallowed a time-release capsule, ensuring that a carefully-regulated comatose state would block out any disturbing memories of my night in my dead mother's bed.

I hovered in the state between wakefulness and sleep. Jumbled associations, day residue (in this case, marmalade jam and a lively discussion about the compositional style of Ramos de Pareja), Mother choking, turning blue, the take-out menu for Seven Happiness, impossible to refold, *Byrd one brere* on the harpsichord, Mrs. Hildebrandt and Mother engaged in a macabre dance, ring around the rosy, *ashes, ashes, we all fall down.* I was not certain whether I was sleeping, dreaming, or merely experiencing one of the side effects prominently discussed in the medication's packaging (MAY LEAD TO HALLUCINATORY PHENOMENA), had I thoroughly reviewed the insert

(SIDE EFFECTS INCLUDE STROKE, SLEEPWALKING, LOSS OF MUSCULAR CONTROL AND DIFFICULTIES SWALLOWING; IF YOU EXPERIENCE ANY OF THE ABOVE, DISCONTINUE USE IMMEDIATELY AND CALL YOUR DOCTOR).

I heard Piccolo get out of bed, stumble in the hallway, searching for illumination. *Mal occhio*, I heard him curse. Where is the light?

"Just outside the bathroom door, my friend," I murmured.

"I am sniffling already" he lamented. "This terrible recirculated air in the plane. Did I disturb you?" He peered inside the room.

"No, my friend," I assured him. I stuffed the pillow under my head and tried, once more, to achieve somnolence. The opiates warned DO NOT TAKE MORE THAN THREE, presumably an advisory against overdose and respiratory slowdown, *viz.* the tendency of one high on barbiturates to forget to breathe.

I trusted that the time-release capsules, designed to circulate steadily in the bloodstream so as to achieve maximum soporific effect, would at some point kick in; that I would stop counting sheep, or the equivalent for a professor of medieval music, analyzing the polyphonic motet structure of the Roman de Fauvel (*fau vel* = veiled lie).

In the crepuscular twilight I prayed. Yes, I prayed: *Credo in Deum, Patrem Omnipotentem*, Welcome Us into Your Light, O Lord and Redeemer. The monotonous refrains, the melismatic flourishes, the sacred incantations. And by dawn's light, I was snoring.

I awoke just before noon, startled by the telephone. Our fellow seminar participants had arrived on the red eye. They had cleared customs, and were en route to the West Side Best Western.

"Everyone is here, it seems." I coughed into my fist.

"I made a frittata," Piccolo offered, peering into the room. He was wearing Mother's apron.

"Thank, you," I said. I threw open the window, riffling the curtain.

"Did I hear you murmuring the Roman de Fauvel?" Piccolo inquired.

"Yes," I stammered. "I tend to recite it when unable to sleep."

"I am a light sleeper myself," he empathized. He confessed that he rose frequently in the middle of the night to relieve his bladder, to flip through the pages of a magazine, to work on a lute arrangement for a popular tune. He worried for his sanity, reading somewhere-or-other (likely one of the magazines he perused while unable to sleep) that lack of sleep, over time, led to psychosis.

"Try one of these," I offered. There was no sense in hoarding my amber bottle of time-release capsules. Piccolo squinted at the label, trying to sound out the chemically loaded name.

"SOLILOQUIL," I offered. If the horse pill could work on me, it certainly had potential for the compact, nervous Piccolo. "I only mention it by way of suggestion."

"So sorry to hear about your Momma," Piccolo sighed.

"Thank you, my friend," I replied. It had been eight-and-a-half months since the fateful incident, since the memorial at M. & Sons Funeraral Chapel, one-stop service (We farm out for cremation and offer a fine brass commemorative urn for your loved one's ashes. Not what you want? Then let me show you the Eternal Bronze line of interment products. . .); since the receipt, during summer break, of artfully arranged baskets from the Manhattan Fruitier (Let's not ruin your diet during this difficult time! Have a pomegranate!), *From*

Your Colleagues at the Department of Music, We're Sorry for Your Loss; since I had collapsed, dizzy, on the floor of the apartment, unable to see the world without Mother in it, all of it a-jumble.

"I'm sorry I didn't say anything earlier. I just found out from Wilhelm."

"No need to be sorry. It's just difficult to talk about it." The survivor, in the days and months following loss, has difficulty acknowledging the brute fact of death. He stumbles around, unable to process input, to sort left from right, up from down. None of it makes sense. The fundamental assumptions have been changed: no longer can he calculate, if x, then y, if y then z. His mind has stopped processing. He cannot take in any more: the howling colors, the buzz of florescent lights; he is unable to stand on his own two feet, *Please sign here to allow transport of the body to the funeral home*. His heart palpates with grief, the absence of the loved one, silence for the duration of the measure.

"A toast to your Momma!" Piccolo shouted. He had found the bottle of Peach Schnapps hidden under the sofa cushion.

"Yes," I said, a tear appearing in my eye. "A toast to Mother." A woman who grew up on the banks of the River Rhine, who frolicked in mountain pastures and played in the *Bayerischer Wald*; a woman who preferred *Die Meistersingers* to the popular music of the day; a woman who had been abandoned by my father one day, without a note or explanation, left to make her own assumptions; a woman who listened, nightly, to the operas of Richard Wagner, claiming that in music transcendence was to be found, moreso than in the communion wafer or a stein of bier. Music the one and only salvation; music the only premonition or reasonable approximation we have of the divine.

"Let us dedicate Machaut to your mother!" Piccolo exclaimed.

> *Se vous n'estes pour mon guerredon née,*
> *Dame, mar vi vo dous regart riant.*
> *Jamais ne mie joie guerredon née,*
> *Qui me fera morir en guerriant.*

38.

Our friend Schlanger wandered into a "gentlemen's club" on the far west side, not to be seen nor heard from since. A search party, consisting of myself, Piccolo, and Wilhelm Helmut-schutter, set off to find him.

The club – The Diamond Lounge, catering to the Distinguished Gentleman of Means – was shuttered during the daylight hours. A custodian – in tense-mixed, broken English – here I try to piece together the linguistic fragments – informed us that a "*loco* man" was on the premises the night before, drinking rum cocktails known as *Adios motherfuckers*, stuffing Euros into the dancers' underwear, and trying to broker an arrangement whereby several of the dancers would return to the Best Western to entertain a "convention," described as a "medieval fraternal brotherhood." He had no idea where the gentleman had gone to.

From there, we scoured the West Village, the East Village, SoHo and NoHo, hoping to find Schlanger passed out on a park bench, ensconced on a seat in a cheap dive bar, or searching for the entrance to a medieval dungeon. We wandered into several churches – the Irish church on Avenue B, the Polish church on Avenue C, the Ukrainian church on Avenue D – anything with a nave and a pipe organ. (The organs in the New World were tuned in the equal temperament; the medieval fervor for the mean-tone and other irregular temperaments, alas, had never reached these shores.)

According to a detective at the precinct (SH. SHLANG. SCHOLONGER. COULD YOU REPEAT THAT?), it was too early to file a missing persons report. He suggested that we look for our friend "under a rock somewhere," ending with the ubiquitous American tag-line, *Have a nice day!*

I suggested that we go to the Hairy Monk for a refreshment. Schlanger might show up, remembering that we had once hoisted pints there, played darts and *name that medieval tune.* He might recognize the basement entrance, the flickering neon sign (*AIRY M*NK), the barmaids with nose rings and facial piercings, majors in sociology and contemporary women's studies. We stumbled inside, exhausted.

"Good to see you, Professor!" shouted the barkeep over the din.

"Good to see you, my man." I led my pack of medieval and Renaissance musicians down the steps and into the low-ceilinged space.

"I like the atmosphere," Wilhelm grunted.

"Yes," Piccolo assented.

"Barkeep, a round for my friends, please."

"He has never been gone this long," Wilhelm fretted. The group was accustomed to Schlanger's forays – pilgrimages to the headquarters of the Hell's Angels; stumblings about Eighth Street looking for "jamba juice"; the annual rite of tattooing, at a parlor just down the block, where his flaccid bicep was branded with fanciful beasts and Latinate phrases. But he had never disappeared for twenty-four hours without a word, without so much as a drunken telephone call.

"What can we do?" I asked. I had learned, over the course of the last year, that we have no control over externalities, that life is a divertimento, a caprice, not a rigidly-constructed sonata with a predictable A-B-A section. Like Brahms' unfinished symphony, it seems to go somewhere, to have an overarching purpose, only to end abruptly mid-movement, after an agonizing slow section. Who knows on any given day whether he will have to dial the fateful numbers 9-1-1, to state the *nature of the emergency.* Whether he will find himself in conversation with the amiable mortician Mr. M., cowering in a windowless room, not wanting to say his final goodbyes to the body in the casket (no matter how skillfully presented and preserved by the crack staff at the funeral home).

In view of the fact that there was nothing to do, nothing save to pray for the best and hope that at some point Schlanger might wander into the pub, I recommended that we order another round, and recite the *Gloria Patri* in canonical form.

Wilhelm informed us that he had finally, after ten years, found a publisher for his groundbreaking work on the Roman de Fauvel. "That's wonderful!" I boomed. I myself had authored but three meager tomes: *Pre-Mensural Notation*, published by the university press (one of the few perks of being an underpaid, untenured professor in an obscure discipline); the others published by a renegade press out of Hamburg, a tiny outfit that published "incendiary work" on topics "too dangerous to suppress," of which my diatribe against the equal temperament apparently qualified.

"To publishing! To Wilhelm! To Luther!" We clinked our mugs.

"The tension in my calf muscle is g-g-gone!" Piccolo squealed.

"Let me propose a toast!" I said. "To period musicians! Those keepers of the flame! Whosoever knows the difference between a Just and an equal-tempered interval, a diurnal comma and a Pythagorean one. To the sacred ratios as they were meant to be heard!"

"Here, here!" my companions joined in. Several rounds later, Piccolo stood on the table, baying a tune, de Machaut's *De bonté, de valour.*

I lost count of how many pitchers we consumed, how many versions of the *Lament of Rachel* we performed in three parts, how many classics of the sixties and seventies we belted to the heavens, fingers flying over air guitars. One day, someone would tear down the Hairy Monk, remove the quaint bric-a-brac and the sketches of the bar's namesake, the rotund belching friar, but for now we were here, for now we lived and breathed and formed somewhat lucid phrases, sang remarkably in tune, and regaled the assembled with an impromptu enactment of the medieval drama, *Slaughter of the Innocents.*

Was there even a heaven? The afterlife trumpeted in magnificats and Gloria Patri? The blinding light and the brass instrumentals, five centuries' worth of monophonic plainchant and melismatic organum, *In nomine Patris, Filli et Spiritus Sancti.* Or was it a figment, a dreamt-up ending, all to avoid the inevitable, subdominant, dominant to tonic, Amen?

Schlanger wandered in mid-verse. He was wearing the same breeches as the night before, but had traded sweater vest for a studded leather riding harness.

"Can it be? Can it be?" he repeated, dumbfounded to have stumbled upon us. "What are you wearing?" Piccolo interjected.

He had no memory of the night before, only a sketchy apprehension that he had been locked in a closet somewhere, a ball gag inserted in this mouth; his pocket contained an itemized receipt from *SM Tannery – West Village,* fine custom-made torture gear, fully refundable if returned within ten days of purchase.

Years as a flagellant, in the abbey at St. Joseph de Clairval, had inured him to pain, made him indifferent to tattooing needles, tongue piercings, nipple clamps, studded dog collars, etc. Years in a monastery, among farm animals and monks who thought the physical body nothing more than a putrid bag of skin and bones, subservient of the immortal soul, had instilled in him a laxity about bathing and personal hygiene. "What does it matter if I smell like a sow?" he was fond of remarking, on the one hand, while wondering, on the other, why the female sex seemed to avoid him.

"I believe this to be a device for restraining beasts of burden, with some flourishes," Wilhelm speculated.

"It does have the appearance of a harness," I concurred, "with silver studs and an attached ball gag." I pointed to the bright red ball dangling from a string.

Schlanger shrugged it off. "It is what it is," he sighed. "Another pitcher," he signaled the barman.

We would spend a week together, clinking glasses and singing four-part polyphony; we would attend lectures on the Roman de Fauvel, and, the week's highlight, an archicembalo performance by the world's only known virtuoso of the instrument, a former friar from Brattleboro, Vermont; we would part, say our *adieux*; none save I knew it was the last time we would convene on these shores (I would send an e-mail afterward, communicating the university's decision to eliminate the symposium from the budget, citing a lack of interest in medieval and Renaissance disciplines); they would return to their medieval towers, their warren-like offices, their temperature-controlled archives, Piccolo to a sad second shift as a wandering lute player; likely, we would never see each other again, not unless a sponsor on the order of King Ludwig II of Bavaria rose from the grave. But for now we were together, for now the beer flowed freely, the sounds of sixties' and seventies' rock anthems filled the pub – seven minutes, eight minutes, the seventeen-minute long *Inna Gadda Davida*. To this weekend. To this night at the Hairy Monk. To a solution to the von Blankenburg problem. To finding a publisher for *Proscribed Intervals*, Wilhelm's tract on Leonin and Peronin, the authors of Wolfenbüttel I. To Piccolo, who pocketed the telephone number of a co-ed dancing on the bar to *What's Your Name, Little Girl?* To Schlanger, who was chomping at the bit.

To the Just and sacred ratios, evidence of the aural truth, music as it was meant to be heard, before Rameau and his kind became intent on splitting the octave into equidistant intervals, each representing 1.25992 of the whole, an inauspicious and cumbersome ratio if ever there was one. To the howling wolfe, the dissonance inherent in every perfect construct.

Shortly after two in the morning (following the departure of a group of amiable co-eds who had enlisted our help in deciphering the lyric to *My Sharona*), we stumbled out of the pub. Piccolo promised to call his *inamorata*. I hailed a taxi, stuffing Schlanger in the backseat before the driver could take note of his fetish gear. "Try to keep him quiet," I instructed Wilhelm, before sending them back to the Best Western.

"Piccolo, it's just you and me," I said, putting my arm around his shoulder. "Are you up to walking home?" I asked.

"Yes," he concurred. "The night is beautiful." We walked up Third Avenue, past the pubs and the taverns, past the place where Rolf's once stood, the desolate corner of Third and Twenty-Sixth, the *trompe l'oeil* of the enchanted forest, the murals of the Zugspitze, left now to the rubble of memory.

I wiped a tear from my eye and pressed on.

39.

The next day, we had a full lecture program: Campagnoli's *Nuovo Methodo della Mecanica Progressiva: Evidence of a Parallel Tradition*; *Everything You Wanted to Know About the Quarter Comma Meantone But Were Afraid to Ask: Don't be Afraid of the Wolfe!*; *Galin-Paris Cheve: The "New" Way?* Participants congregated in the halls during breaks, where they enjoyed lukewarm coffee and nibbled on unevenly-warmed miniature *quiche*.

Schlanger perked up mid-afternoon, sometime during the lecture on *Versuch einer grundlichen Violinschule*. It was not until the odious Louis Spohr, in 1832, published his incendiary tome *Violinschule*, that we see the equal temperament ("gleichschebenden") heralded as the "only" tuning system; by 1885, when Ellis performed his diabolical computations, according 100 cents per semi-tone, the damage had been done, irreparable.

"Ja, ja," Shlanger murmured, before lapsing once more into a profound sleep.

"Should we wake him?" Piccolo asked.

"No, he needs his rest." Fred's Cantina did not have enough biscuits or bread crusts to soak up the turmoil of the night before.

I envied his ability to sleep soundly, on a cramped writing desk.

"I tried the SOLILOQUIL last night." Piccolo elbowed me. "It was very effective."

"I'm glad to hear it." I was down to the last few pills, cutting them in half so as to prolong my supply.

"Wilhelm says Schlanger babbles in his sleep. Recites *Ine gesach die heide*, in medieval German. He murmured something about a dungeon on the Lower East Side. About a dominant named Lola."

The lecturer scuffed a chair at the conclusion of the program to let the audience know it was time to wake up. Participants greeted me and slapped me on the back (awkwardly: we were most of us pale and flaccid creatures) for a job well done. *Where is Ernst?* I was asked, more than once, a reference to our dear brother at the University of Hamburg, he who had embraced the equal temperament, gone to the dark side, the place of toneless, soulless, enharmonic equivalents.

"Ernst had other commitments this year," I said, omitting mention of his treachery, his malign missives, his slanderous accusations about Schlanger, his "firmly-held belief" that we were propagators of a lost cause, obsessed with the sacred ratios, foolishly convinced that 3:2, infinitely multiplied, would yield a sonorous solution to the problem of tonality.

They would learn, soon enough. Ernst's scurrilous diatribe against the mean-tone was scheduled to be published in the fall – not by Musica Antiqua, the usual university publishers of obscure musicological musings, but by Norton & Sons, a giant publishing conglomerate. It would be available in commercial establishments for a reasonable price, not the exorbitant rate we professors extracted from captive students – Buy this book on the syllabus or else! – in university bookstores. I had read excerpts from the book. A chapter advocating that *The Well-Tempered Clavier*, by Bach senior, was the opening salvo in the equal-tempered movement. A particularly vitriolic section on Zarlino's sonorous number. A fawning appraisal of Alexander Ellis' *On the Sensations of Tone*; a disavowal, wholly and completely, of musical tradition antedating the Baroque. The Renaissance oeuvre dismissed with epithets like "unusable," "misbegotten tonalities," and "howling wolves."

"Otto," I shook him. "Will you be well for dinner?"

"Are we going to the Bearded Mendicant?" he asked.

"The Hairy Monk? No, they serve only bar snacks. Chips, pretzels and salted peanuts. We are going to an Italian restaurant with a perambulating violinist."

40.

That night we had dinner at Ciao Napoli, an Italian restaurant in the West Village. A three-course prix fixe meal: a small garden salad (carrot shavings, a mostly vinegar *vinaigrette*), followed by pasta Bolognese (meatballs extra), and tiramisu for dessert. House wine by the jug.

I welcomed the symposium participants, thanking them for their dedication to our dwindling field of study and for making the arduous journey to the States. Schlanger toasted the assembled and the day when "the mean-tone is recognized as the true musical standard." Yves de Couchet informed us of a period music revival in the Alsace region. After five years of assiduously trying to locate a publisher, Madrigal Books was set to publish Jacques' tome on Early Sources of Organum. It had received the imprimatur of the Collegium of Early Music, a necessary distinction if a work of scholarship is to find circulation outside of academe.

For fifteen years we had congregated, celebrated these achievements. We shared insights regarding the centuries' long attempt to split the octave, the philosophical strife occasioned by the endeavor. We played in intimate settings the instruments of the era, the lute and lira da braccia, the virginal and harpsichord, the clavicytherium. Early Music as it was meant to be heard, Just and pure.

"The equal temperament is a scourge!" Schlanger bellowed, sounding like Zarlino railing against his arch-rival Galilei. "How can we accept this trampling of the mystical ratios? This perversion of sound relationships in the interest of uniformity? How does the modern ear accept this abomination?" He let the linguine untwirl into the plate. "And now this betrayal by Ernst! Siding with the treasonous Sporh and Alexander Ellis?! He writes commentaries in *Musicology* mocking us for our intransigence. He dismisses us as delusional madmen! He makes fun of our experiments with the mesolabium. Disparages your year-long study of the monks from Solesmes [he pointed to Jacques St. Jacques]." Schlanger ripped a piece of bread from the loaf and stuffed it in his mouth. "Ernst is a pox upon us. A scourge. A sell-out. We need to publicly disavow him." He pounded on the table. "Take this." He handed me a leaky ballpoint from the West Side Best Western.

We, the assembled, historians of medieval and Renaissance music, players of period instruments, proponents of the mean-tone and shifting temperaments, do hereby proclaim the following:

We believe in the perfect ratios, Ptolemy's theory of the harmony of the spheres;

We believe, like the sixteenth-century theorist Pietro Aron, that the octave "releases all possible consonances like a fertile mother," that the ratios of 4:3 and 3:2 are divinely inspired, the numerical correlates of an ordered universe;

We believe that these principles, divine and Just, are reflected in the proportions of the universe itself, in the elliptical orbits of planets, the reverberations of a string, the oscillating overtones of a struck note;

Like our predecessors, Guido d'Arezzo and Boeuthius, we refuse to believe that the solution to the problem of temperament lies in tampering with the sacred ratios;

We will uncover the real truth, not the 'truth' as propagated in On the Sensations of Tone [here the pen, a cheap ball point emblazoned with the name of the residence inn, began to gob up]

We reject Alexander Ellis and all his works, the scurrilous Rameau, William Braid White, propagators of unholy truths, sham musical realities, artificial tonalities, corrupt musical practices;

Ernst, oh vile traitor, ye who abandoned your brethren for an equidistant solution to one of the greatest conundrums of history. . . You deserve fifty lashings, an eternity as the apprentice of Carlo Gesualdo. . .

Here, Otto stopped dictating and fell off the chair. The *maître d'* came running. "Are you okay, Sir? Are you okay?" he asked, peering into his eyes.

Otto, flat on his back, slightly concussed, waved him off. "I'm all right. It's all right," he said, struggling to compose himself.

No doubt someone in the back of the restaurant was calling a lawyer, ascertaining the extent of the establishment's liability for failing to prevent an intoxicated patron from climbing atop a chair, delivering a manifesto against the equal temperament, and falling backward onto an unprotected hard surface. Should the restaurant have stopped the flow of house wine earlier? Should they have weighted the chairs, a flimsy rattan variety easily capable of tipping over? Could they have foreseen that a drunken patron would stand atop the chair to rail against the *gleichschebenden*, and incidentally to heckle the violinist? Could they have known that he would topple over, hit the uncarpeted floor, causing a momentary – seconds, really – lapse of consciousness? I had contributed to this backlog of senseless lawsuits. Litigation seeking to assign blame, to point a finger, to apportion fault via convenient percentages. To absolve ourselves of our own, stupid culpability.

"Do you want to call the ambulance?" the *maître d'* asked.

"No, it's not necessary," Schlanger said, wiping the froth from his lips and sitting down.

"The tiramisu is on the house," the *maître d'* offered. A member of the staff mopped up the floor.

"Thank you, that's very kind of you," I replied. "My friend apologizes for his, um, effusive behavior."

"No apologies necessary, Sir," he responded. "I insist. The tiramisu is delicious. I highly recommend it. At least have some biscotti. Almond-flavored. Very delicious."

Fear not, Ciao Napoli, with your murals of the Amalfi coast, your *faux* oil paintings of Renaissance masters, your wine bottles dripping with candlewax. We have no desire to sue you, to hold you liable for the rantings of our esteemed colleague or his *thwack* on the floor; we have no desire to haul Ciao Napoli, est. 1977, into a court of law, to fault our poor waiter for liberally pouring the house wine, for failing to prevent our colleague from mounting the chair and falling backward onto the floor. We will gather our things and be on our way. Thank you kindly for your hospitality.

I took one of Otto's arms, Piccolo the other, and we dragged him out of the establishment. *Thwack, thwack, thwack,* his shins hit the steps leading to the pavement. The air was misty, vaporous, threatening rain.

"What are we going to do next?" they asked. Otto hung between us.

"I think we've had enough excitement for the night," I said. "Let's reconvene in the morning." Piccolo and I threw our inebriated colleague into a taxi and went home.

41.

On Sunday, I had scheduled the highlight of the symposium: a performance by Hillare de Roquefalaise, archicembalo virtuoso. Former Trappist monk and maker of quality rum cakes.

In the quiet confines of the monastery, isolated from the outer world, Hillare heard natural reverberations. The wind in the cracks of the window, the bees in the rose garden, the *hush* of empty spaces in the chapel. He was able to identify not only half or whole tone, but infinitesimal pitches within these steps, imponderable ratios that had been described by the ancient philosophers. He applied his gift to a dulcimer that had been lying around the monastery, after receiving assurances that music making was not prohibited by his vow of silence. His ear, sensitive to aural nuances, soon realized that tones existed which could not be replicated on any modern keyboard. Immersion in books on medieval history alerted him to the existence of the archicembalo. It was the invention of Nicola Vincentino, an Italian and enthusiast of the Greek philosophers, a man who desired to construct an instrument that could replicate every key according to the Pythagorean ratios, without compromise or omission. The archicembalo had rows of black keys corresponding to the omitted half-steps, or missing accidentals. Hillare de Roquefalaise devoted himself to study of the odd instrument and mastery of its cumbersome disposition; he had the necessary dexterity, a wide finger span, and digits so excruciatingly slender that they could slip within the successive rows of black keys, finding the perfect tone.

Schlanger placed an annual order with *The Friar's Rumcake* and only later learned of the cake maker's avocation. To our knowledge, Hillare was the world's only virtuoso of the instrument; to most, the instrument was a curiosity, representing man's aspiration to replicate the infinite number of tones in the spectrum.

The divine ratios, in his view, were proof positive of the existence of a Superior Being – why else did the planetary orbits correspond to the divine proportions? How could the semi-tone correspond to the ratio 1.25992, as the equal temperament posited – what was, after all, an irrational number?

The archicembalo was tuned according to Zarlino's scenario, or sonorous number. Zarlino had extrapolated from Pythagoras the proportions for the major third, the minor third and the major sixth, ratios based on the mystical number six.

The room bristled with excitement. As professors of medieval and Renaissance music we were of course familiar with split-key variants such as the archicembalo, instruments with several rows of keys and rather awkward dispositions. These were oddities in the annals of instrument building, representing theoretical aspirations rather than practical considerations.

Hillare took the bench, performing several of Machaut's ballades, including *Mes Esperis* and *Si vous n'estes*. He concluded with *Ma fin est mon commencement*. It is one of Machaut's best known works, a rondeau in retrograde motion. The second section is a repetition of the first, with the voices inverted. In this way we begin with the end and end with the beginning.

Ma fin est mon commencement echoed in my head. I thought of Mother, who was no longer here but perhaps existed somewhere, in a realm beyond apprehension. I thought of the circle of fifths, perfect mathematical ratios that could not be reconciled with the empirical data, the misbegotten fifth and life's unaccountable imperfections. The way time, which I was accustomed to counting as a musician, duple or triple meter, accent on the downbeat, was something you could step out of, *Hello, my mother's stopped breathing, she's choking on a wonton, please come quickly.* When the music resumed, *You'll learn to acclimate to life without her, please sign here to authorize the funeral expenses,* life would go on, *poco a poco.* Though you resisted like a stuck key, a deadened tone, the refrain would repeat: *Se vous n'estes.*

All that is lost and nevermore.

My colleagues dispersed to their universities, their medieval hamlets, the shires where they studied illuminated manuscripts and dismantled organ pipes, searching for the mystical sonorities.

I was reluctant to bid *adieu* to Piccolo. I had grown accustomed to his presence in the apartment. At night we would perform duets, simple strophes, the apartment resonating with the fourteenth century melodies of *les trouvères pastourelles.*

Our favorite, *Dous Amis*:
My friends, hear my complaint:
To you laments
And complains,
For want of your succor,
My whole self, whom love so compelled,
That I am held fast,

From which I have great pain,
When you do not succor me
In my languor;
For otherwise
There is nothing that brings me comfort.
Thus my tears increase every day,

Piccolo was scheduled for the midnight flight to Bologna. I summoned a taxi service to pick him up three hours in advance of departure, so as to allow him enough time to navigate customs, to vomit once or twice in the basin of the washroom (so severe was his anxiety about the prospect of acute air catastrophe), and to strenuously jump in place so as to avert the possibility of deep vein thrombosis.

"I will miss you, my friend."

"I will miss you too," he said, a tear in his eye. "Though I must be traveling on my way now," he said. The infernal New York City humidity was warping the fretboard of his lute and exacerbating post-nasal drip. Though sensitive to the state of our instruments and the quality of their sound – accustomed to making string adjustments, refining tensions, replacing busted nuts and the like – we musicians were frequently at a loss for words, and tone-deaf in matters of emotion.

<h1 style="text-align:center">42.</h1>

Mrs. Hildebrandt having no relations to speak of, the vessel containing her ashes was deeded to the co-op. It was difficult to visualize Mrs. Hildebrandt inside the handsome brass urn with Roman flourishes. It was hard to believe that a grown woman, flesh and blood and bone, had been reduced to several fistfuls of rough sand – which, in morbid fascination, I felt compelled to run my fingers through. Where did she exist, amidst this rubble? (One of Mr. M.'s sons had confided to me that they combed through the "cremains," removing the larger, less combustible bone fragments, the difficult-to-pulverize femur and the thick cranium, so as not to disturb the family members.)

The lawyers for Seven Happiness made an offer, conveyed to me by Ms. La Planta. The figure – $85,000, to be precise – was comparable to recoveries for similar losses involving airway obstruction, and represented a "significant victory," according to my counselor-at-law, since Seven Happiness' agency in mother's death was questionable. This figure would be further reduced by Ms. La Planta's contingency fee, and litigation costs (an expert on standby who was willing to testify that wontons presented a known risk of choking), for a total recovery of $55,000. Having a dollar figure assigned to my loss – which was boundless, a struck note with infinite overtones – seemed obscene.

"I would accept the offer," Ms. La Planta counseled. "The risks of pursuing the litigation are too great, given the weaknesses in the case. Seven Happiness will also agree to dismissal of their countersuit for defamation and tortious interference with business relations."

"I don't know," I hesitated, recalling Mother's first dip in the soup, the uncharacteristic *slurp*.

"The legal theory is shaky," she softened. "I can make it seem like they're a sloppy operation, I can point to the lag in delivery time. But there are considerable obstacles to proving causation, even if we can show that their wontons were, um, gelatinous," she said.

"I know," I acknowledged.

"It's a good recovery," she said. "The most we could hope for under the circumstances." We sat side-by-side in the conference room, no court reporter, *tap-tap-tap*, to transcribe my grief, to record my lamentation. My interlocutor was gone, back to his offices on Long Island with his battered leather case and tabbed file folders. There would be no more sparring, no more question, beat, followed by (move to strike as non-responsive) answer, no more *Please answer the question asked and only the question asked*, no more *Please refrain from speculation*.

The final account of Mother's life and precipitous death had been transcribed by the official court reporter, my responses – frequently long-winded, difficult to punctuate, filled with medieval allusions and anatomical references – the three phases of swallowing, the five stages of grief, *deglutition apnea*, the impossibility of both breathing and swallowing, *schmerzen*, the impossibility of assimilating loss and going on – deciphered by the esteemed court reporter, who did her best with the spellings (F-BOW, hypoglossal?, L-A-R-Y-N-G-E-A-L closure, can you please spell that?).

I hadn't composed a requiem, an isorhythmic motet, or even a simple *trouvère* song, to mark her passing. I hadn't consecrated my grief to some larger purpose, a four-part fugue, or a theme and variations. I hadn't transformed my private agonies via ornamental flourishes, an affecting *largo* section, *subito rubato*, into moving, universal truths. I chose instead to sue Seven Happiness LLC and Bernice Wong, individually, looking to shift blame, to appease my guilt, to apportion fault via convenient percentages (10% delivery man, 70% short-order cook, 20% to Dr. Wong-Goldman for poor dentition), for what was essentially a statistical aberration, a wanton act.

In the end, I accepted the advice of my counselor-at-law. I affixed my signature to the settlement papers, avowing that I had read them thoroughly; and that I had been aided in the endeavor by my attorney of record, with whose services I was thoroughly and completely satisfied. We mutually covenanted to release any and all claims, suits, demands, etc. against one another connected to, arising out of, or in any way related to the incident, and I stipulated to the dismissal of *Luther van der Loon v. Seven Happiness, LLC and Bernice Wong, et al.*, with prejudice.

"Of course, nothing can bring your mother back, Luther. We can just try to redress the legal wrong. I know it's small consolation. You get to the end and there's just a check (I would not, like the hero in a medieval morality play, take a fictional trip to heaven and say hello to her, return to earth, content that she was not moldering somewhere off the Long Island Expressway). "I don't know what to say," the usually eloquent Ms. La Planta fumbled. It was simpler to strenuously object than to offer condolences; easier to joust with the legal dimwit, Stewart

Cushman, Law Offices of Stewart Cushman, P.C., than to acknowledge grievous loss. "It's obvious you loved your mother a lot. That you would do anything for her." (Could she bring back Mother? Could she save Rolf's from demolition? Could she stop the wrecking ball? Her powers were limited.) "I'm truly sorry" she said, placing her red-lacquered fingertips on my arm. "Try to take some time off, if you can. Go on a vacation. St. Bart's is nice this time of year. Get out of this pressure cooker."

I nodded and thanked her for her zealous legal representation. She had wrested a settlement from Seven Happiness, LLC, albeit without an admission of culpability and with onerous provisions precluding me from discussing the terms of the settlement, binding on my heirs and assigns. It was, as she said, a significant "victory," given the lack of proof positive that their wontons were undercooked and inherently dangerous.

I gathered my personal items and left the conference room. The receptionist bid me *adieu*. I declined the offer of a hard candy. Goodbye, Bloodstone & Moore, specialists in personal injury work, *When you're down for the count, we fight for you*, advocates for the injured, the maimed, the bereaved, those cracked beyond recognition, those who find solace in Asiatic Pheasant teacups and scratched recordings of *Die Meistersingers*. I stepped into the vestibule and pressed the down button.

What had I expected? That recounting the particulars of Mother's death – the sudden airway occlusion, the deprivation of oxygen, the soundless terror – would, like a sacred incantation, bring her back? That I could summon her from the Hereafter, contrary to all known laws of physics, to religious teachings concerning the soul's migration, to physiological experiments confirming the irreversibility of brain death? That

I, like Nicola Vincentino, the inventor of the archicembalo, could construct an instrument capable of sounding all of the notes in the aural spectrum, commendable in theory but in practice unworkable? I was vindicated, in the eyes of the law, but I was still bereft, adrift, incapable of finding the notes to express my lamentation.

43.

Mrs. Hildebrandt's apartment was sold, at full market price, to a couple with a squalling infant. *Knock, knock, knock*: please stop playing the harpsichord, little Emily is trying to sleep.

I reconciled myself to teaching group piano to arthritic adults. I started with the two-handed classic, *The Scissors Grinder*, progressing onto *Chord Frolic* and *Long, Long Ago*. None of my students were able to maintain proper finger position, let alone master the rhythms and melodies of these method book classics. The metronome, with its relentless *tock*, counting out the measures, gave way to a more loosely-interpreted notion of time. Time that grew ever expansive as students stumbled over brisk passages or flubbed an unexpected accidental. "Bravo," I clapped at the end of each class, applauding not them, but myself for remaining patient and resisting the urge to deliver unflattering appraisals of their talents into their hearing aids.

Passing by Shakespeare & Co. on Lower Broadway, I noticed prominently displayed in the shop window Ernst's book, *The Battle for the Soul of Music: The Equal-Tempered Revolution*.

"The author will be speaking here next month," a shop clerk cheerfully informed me, publication of the book coinciding with the birthday of John-Philippe Rameau, propagator of heretical tonalities and bestial falsehoods about his fellow musical theorist, Zarlino.

"Duly noted," I said. Ernst had dedicated his book to the fifteenth and sixteenth century advocates of the equal temperament, those souls brave enough to question Pythagorean wisdom, to risk ridicule by Ptolemy, seeing, in Rameau's defiance, a "radical foresightedness" and "prescience about the evolution of music towards the vertical, rather than the horizontal, towards harmonic complexity."

"Would you like to purchase a copy?" the clerk inquired, taking note of my unseemly interest in medieval music and in the exploits of Carlos Gesualdo, depraved compositional genius, to whom an entire chapter had been devoted.

"No," I rejoined. I had no desire to line the coffers of Norton & Sons, world-wide publishing conglomerate, with proceeds from my pitiable salary. I, a Pythagorean purist, would never concede that splitting the octave into equidistant steps was the only means of reconciling the dissonances inherent in the circle of fifths.

Feeling guilty about how much time the clerk had spent with me discussing *The Battle for the Soul of Music*, I felt compelled to purchase something, settling on a copy of *The Sun Also Rises* from a neighboring table.

"I'll take this," I said, dashing out the door.

44.

Seven Happiness shuttered its Second Avenue franchise, citing negative publicity and a decline in profits occasioned by my "frivolous" lawsuit. I could not pass by the desolate storefront, or bring myself to eat take-out Chinese.

"You can't go on like this," Cecilia said. "Why don't you let me help you?"

Were I not to surmount this last, final hurdle, I would remain a mental prisoner, my take-out options severely delimited. I would forever associate Chinese take-out with death, questionable cooking methods, and the futility of advertised life-saving procedures.

"Very well."

She had me imagine placing an order (*I'd like wonton soup, please, with shrimp fried rice and cashew chicken*), anticipating its arrival.

Open the bag, she directed. I imagined myself consuming the broth, encountering the wonton. *Feel its texture on your tongue*, Cecilia prompted me, trying to make the experience banal, strip it of its associative meaning, time-honored techniques of cognitive behavioral therapy. *Now swallow the wonton*, she commanded, and after several practice sessions in which I choked up and was unable to proceed further, I finally succeeded in "swallowing" the agent of my mother's destruction.

"Bravo," she said.

The next day, we ordered in from Charlie's Sichuan. In the wake of Seven Happiness' closure, they had picked up the greater part of the take-out commerce in the delivery radius, notwithstanding complaints about MSG-induced migraines and the sad state of their Peking duck. *Breathe in deeply*, Cecilia counseled, taking note of my pallid complexion and clammy hands, commonplace signs of anxiety in the grief-stricken and the bereft. "I don't think I can do it," I said, panicking, words sticking in my throat.

In the interregnum between placing the order (*extra duck sauce please; hold the plastic utensils, we'd like to go green!*) and its arrival, I went from anxious anticipation to full-scale panic attack.

When Jose buzzed to inform that our take-out had arrived, I nearly collapsed on the floor, the dread intolerable, notwithstanding my efforts at positive visualization, obsessive repetition of my mantra, *You have the power, you can do it.*

"You've already been through it in your head. You'll be fine." Cecilia paid the deliveryman and carried the bag into the kitchen, where she unpacked the contents. Fried rice, cashew chicken, beef and broccoli, innumerable packets of duck sauce, plastic utensils (so much for *Go green!*), and finally, the container of wonton soup. The focal point of my rage, the basis for all of my colorful accusations about Seven Happiness and Bernice Wong *et al.*

"I'm going to remove the lid," she said. I felt the onslaught of steam, the overwhelming scent of lye paste.

"Now sit down."

My hands shook as I attempted to separate the chopsticks. "Just use a spoon," Cecilia counseled. I ventured into the murky broth. My rate of respiration increased. *You're fine, you can do this*, I told myself, summoning the positive energy of my visual rehearsals. *You can do this, swallowing is an autonomic reflex, wonton soup does not possess magical properties.*

"It's okay, Luther. You're okay," Cecilia encouraged me, sitting close by, presumably to perform the Heimlich maneuver in the event things went other than as anticipated.

I hesitated, abandoning the spoon on the side of the bowl.

"Perhaps it might be better to use the chopsticks?" I asked, rationalizing rather than confronting my fear, my terror at the unknown. The prospect that life might be snuffed out in an instant, owing to a fatal confluence of boy choy and wontons.

"You can do it."

"Cecilia, I just don't know if I'm ready," I pleaded. *Do not force me to cross this final, therapeutic threshold, but allow me to linger a while longer in denial or depression, to savor a fruit of the month.*

"You're ready," Cecilia said. My hand shook violently, causing ripples in the broth.

"It's only soup. It doesn't have magical properties," she reminded me.

I attempted to calm my nerves, drawing on my experience as a period performer and virtuoso interpreter of the *trouvère* repertoire. Deep breath, steady hands.

A wonton folded in the Shanghai style, lye paste and water, nothing more.

The universe will not smite me for daring to eat wonton soup.

The odds of succumbing to the same Fate as Mother were a billion to one, greater than those of being flattened in the crosswalk on Second Avenue (reality testing).

In consuming wonton soup I was in no way dishonoring Mother's memory, committing a sacrilege, or sanctioning negligent food handling practices.

Life is an irreducible equation; it is not a waltz with a predictable A-B-A section; its ending may take us by surprise, terminating, mid-measure, before the chord can resolve.

I felt the texture of the wonton on my tongue. I held it there a while (Cecilia stood at the ready, uncertain as to whether I was reliving the fatal FBAO, or merely procrastinating), contemplating all of the possibilities, life or death, laughter or emergency evacuation procedures. An interminable cadence, *subito rubato*.

"Swallow," Cecilia urged, sensing in me more than the usual amount of therapeutic resistance.

Swallowing: A miraculous coordination of the oropharynx, nasopharynx. Temporary cessation of breathing. From there, the rhythmic contractions of the epiglottis, *viz.*, peristalsis, propel the bolus into the unknown.

It was Mother who insisted, that fateful July day, that we order from Seven Happiness Chinese take-out. It was she, not I, who decided upon the restaurant, she who chose General Tso, one of the dinner specials, despite my savage critiques of the orange glaze and my warnings, unheeded, that the sesame seeds would become stuck in her teeth, necessitating an emergency visit to Dr. Wong-Goldman. My *ex-post facto* reconstructions of the event, my self-excoriations, my (Cecilia would say) obsessive reliving of the incident, leave out this crucial fact.

I see now that my guilt dreams, the recurring imagery of impossible-to-fold take-out menus and posters for *How to render aid to a choking victim* – cannot simply be deemed the expressions of a weighted conscience. For I was not to blame for the lax cooking practices of a Chinese take-out establishment plagued by health code violations. But I would rather view myself as a culpable participant, an oaf incapable of performing basic life-saving procedures, than accept the notion that we dwell in a random and senseless universe. A universe in which an otherwise robust woman, without forewarning or at least an ominous chord, signaling the listener to a shift in the mood, could die suddenly, after choking on a wonton.

She loved me, and I her: a perfect consonance. Somewhere, in the deep silences, her soul, her projection, her spiritual aspect, vibrates sympathetically. I swallowed, telling myself *You're okay, you're okay, let it go*, letting the wonton slide backwards into the unknown.

"You did it! You did it!" Cecilia exclaimed.

45.

The Pythagorean proportions – the mystical ratios of 3:2 (the fifth), 4:3 (the fourth) and 2:1 (the octave) – were for years the unassailable foundation of Western music. Ratios inscribed in the elliptical motion of the planets; numbers in some sense divine. For centuries, the finest minds – astronomers, astrologists, musicians, theorists – pondered the riddle of the circle of fifths. Why was it that the circle did not end on C, where it had begun, but fell somewhere short, ending on a diminished fifth, a hideous augmented fourth, otherwise known as the "wolfe"? How was this imperfection possible in a world that obeyed the sacred concordances? This conundrum occupied some of the greatest minds in history, spurring the vitriolic correspondence between theorists like Gioseffo Zarlino and his treacherous pupil Vincenzo Galilei, who published anonymous tracts disparaging his teacher's works.

These debates, with their cosmic overtones, no longer concern us. In the nineteenth century, the equal temperament eventually eclipsed any other form of regular or irregular temperament. The equal temperament enabled orchestral playing, enharmonic modulation, and ensured uniformity of tone. It was, in the words of my arch-nemesis, Professor Ernst, Distinguished Professor, Holder of the Rameau Chair at the University of Hamburg, inevitable. Nineteenth-century composition, with its richness of sonorities, its emphasis on harmonic progression, would never have been possible in the mean-tone, in which only five of the keys were workable. The rules of counterpoint – those rules which had enabled music to soar despite its harmonic limitations – diminished in importance, as performers rallied around the 440 hZ standard. The distinction between C sharp and D-flat, the diesis, became historical artifact.

What is Just and true, I ask, and what a hideous, tonal compromise?

Acknowledgments

Thanks to Rick Moody, mentor nonpareil, who encouraged me, allowed me to believe in myself, knew what I needed to hear when I needed to hear it, and is possessed of an excess of wisdom and grace at which I can only marvel.

Thanks to Amy Wallen, who schooled me in the nuts-and-bolts of novel building and who is always, unfailingly, right.

Thanks to Phil Schultz, who taught me everything I know about voice.

Thanks to the many others from whom I have learned and who inspire me, to everyone connected in any way with the New York State Summer Writers' Institute, where I was steeped in the art of the word and allowed to flourish. To Leia and to Ev, early cheerleaders of the work, and others who pored over drafts and were exacting in their criticism.

Thanks to the authors of the many books I consulted on the subject of tuning and temperament, among them, Ross W. Duffin, *How Equal Temperament Ruined Harmony*; Stuart Isacoff, *Temperament*; and J. Murray Barbour, *Tuning and Temperament*.

To my boys, one in heaven and one on earth, my reasons for being and mon sang, mon âme.

About the Author

Carol LaHines' fiction has appeared in *Fence, Hayden's Ferry Review, Denver Quarterly, Cimarron Review, The Literary Review, North Dakota Quarterly, South Dakota Review, The South Carolina Review, The Chattahoochee Review, The Nebraska Review, North Atlantic Review, Sycamore Review, Permafrost, redivider, Literary Orphans, Literal Latte*, and elsewhere. Her short story, "Papijack," was selected by judge Patrick Ryan as the recipient of the 2017 Lamar York Prize for Fiction. Her short stories and novellas have also been finalists for the Mary McCarthy Prize from Sarabande Books, the David Nathan Meyerson fiction prize, the *New Letters* short story award, the Pirate's Alley Faulkner Society award, and the Disquiet Literary Prize, among others. She lives in New York City and is a graduate of New York University, Gallatin Division.

9 781949 180916